Some You
Win . . .

Alan Gibbons is a full-time writer and a visiting speaker and lecturer at schools, colleges and literary events nationwide, including the major book festivals: Edinburgh, Northern Children's Book Festival, Swansea, Cheltenham, Sheffield and Salford. Alan has recently embarked on a high profile, nationwide campaign to champion libraries and librarianship and to reevaluate government commitment to educational spending.

Also by Alan Gibbons:

FOOTBALL TITLES
Julie and Me and Michael Owen Makes Three
Total Football series:
Under Pressure
Divided We Fall
Injury Time
Last Man Standing
Power Play
Twin Strikers
Final Countdown

HORROR TITLES
Hell's Underground:
Scared to Death
The Demon Assassin
Renegade
Witch Breed

FANTASY TITLES
The Legendeer Trilogy:
Shadow of the Minotaur
Vampyr Legion
Warriors of the Raven

The Legendeer Trilogy (3-in-1)

The Darkwing:
Rise of the Blood Moon
Setting of a Cruel Sun

The Darkwing Omnibus (2-in-1)

REAL LIFE THRILLERS
The Lost Boys' Appreciation Society
Blood Pressure
The Edge
Caught in the Crossfire
The Defender

Some You Win . . .

Alan Gibbons

Orion
Children's Books

Thanks to Robert Pendleton, Walton and Kirkdale Junior League and
Everton F.C.

First published in Great Britain in 1997
by Orion Children's Books
Reissued in Great Britain in 2010
by Orion Children's Books
a division of the Orion Publishing Group Ltd
Orion House
5 Upper St Martin's Lane
London WC2H 9EA
An Hachette UK company

978-1-4440-0175-4

A catalogue record for this book is available from the British Library.

www.orionbooks.co.uk

PART ONE

Some You Lose

One

Kev made a despairing lunge, but Jelly Wobble was past him. Like a ferret up a rotten drain-pipe, Kev thought gloomily. A big, fat ferret, and the drain-pipe was his side's 18-yard box. Sold the dummy, and by that ugly lump.

'Nail him, Guv!'

'Close him down.'

The shouts of Kev's team-mates were more in desperation than hope, but it was a waste of breath. He was in no position to close anybody down. Seeing the danger from a speculative through-ball too late, he had thrown himself into a sliding tackle that left him floundering in the wake of the heavyweight Blessed Hearts' striker. Where *did* a tub of lard like that get his speed from? He was like jet-propelled tripe with attitude.

'Rats!'

Kev breathed his dismay through thin, chapped lips and struggled to his feet just in time to see Jelly Wobble working a nifty one-two with the only supporting attacker in the box.

'Spread yourself,' came a hoarse adult voice. Their manager, Bobby Jones, was bouncing up and down on the touch-line, bawling his head off. 'Stand big, Joey. Narrow the angle.'

But asking Joey Bannen to stand big was like getting a hippo to bungee-jump. It just wasn't going to happen. Unnerved by the sight of the Blessed Hearts' strike force closing on him, he had gone to ground, a petrified little rabbit facing the foxes over a sea of mud.

It took no more than a lightly-weighted chip to put the ball over the tiny goal-keeper. Kev ground his teeth as the ball slapped the back of the rain-drenched net in a shower of silvery droplets.

Three-nil. Three stinking nil! And the Dog and Gunners were losing to Blessed Hearts of all people.

Kev's past had come back to haunt him good style. Any minute, he thought, any teeth-gnashing minute they'll be over here gloating. Football was meant to be the making of him. He'd promised himself – out of trouble and into glory. Instead, every missed pass, every over-struck cross, every defensive blunder was like a razor cut, reminding him what a no-hoper he was. He just couldn't seem to get his head above water. He closed his eyes against the thin winter sunlight and allowed his head to sag.

'Lost your way a bit then, didn't you, McGovern?'

He gave Jelly Wobble a sullen stare. He'd never liked the lad when they were neighbours back in Kirkdale. Now he detested him. JW was a reminder of a life he'd rather forget, a life that, despite his efforts, had its foot on his neck.

'Shut it, you.'

'Make me.'

It was the wrong thing to say. The taunts could still get to him. Jelly Wobble started smirking all over his creamy moon face. He was revelling in Kev's discomfort.

'You're not worth the effort,' Kev snarled. That's it. Hit him with a superior put-down and arrogant stare down the nose.

But Jelly Wobble wasn't fazed. He had his own line

in put-downs. 'What is it with you anyway, Mc-Govern?' he asked. 'This isn't the sort of match you're usually interested in.'

His fingers were striking imaginary Swan Vestas. Kev stiffened. It was never going to go away, was it? His one big mistake, and there it was, tattooed right across his forehead. Kevin McGovern – fire-raiser.

'It was old man Nolan you torched, wasn't it?'

'It was an accident.'

'Yeah, well you would say that, wouldn't you?'

Kev saw Jamie Moore trotting over to lend a bit of moral support. 'Something up?'

'Ask him,' said Jelly Wobble, making his way back to the centre circle. 'We go way back, don't we, Mc-Govern?'

'What was all that about?' asked Jamie.

'Just a slimeball with a big mouth.'

'But what exactly was the slimeball mouthing off *about*?'

Kev was getting a rush of prickles down his back and neck. 'The time I got into trouble,' he said. 'Last summer.'

'Oh.' Jamie looked troubled for a moment. For ages his parents had forbidden him to knock around with Kev because of the smell of danger that hung round him. It was only in the last week or so that they had changed their minds. It seemed Kev was finally out of the leper colony, on account of his being a reformed character. Well, that was the story.

'The feller who died, you mean?' Jamie asked. 'So how does the fat kid know what happened?'

'See this lot?' Kevin explained, indicating the opposition. 'I know them. They're lads from the estate I used to live on before we moved to the Diamond. Jelly Wobble lived round the corner from me.'

'You could have told me!' said Jamie.

'I thought of giving this morning a miss altogether,' said Kev. 'I wish I had done.'

'Oh well,' said Jamie. 'At least I know why they've been paying you so much attention.'

Kev nodded ruefully. 'They've been on my back since they clocked me in the changing rooms. Anyway, let's talk about it later. There's a game to pull out of the fire.'

Gordon Jones had just rolled the ball to John O'Hara to re-start the match. John took stock of play and lofted it towards Kev as he crossed the halfway line.

'Guv,' John shouted. 'On to Ant.'

Kev smiled. Anthony Glover was Ant because of the way the lads said his name – Ant Knee. And because he scurried round the football pitch as if he had three pairs of legs.

'Guv, Guv,' he called, running into space.

Kev brought the ball down expertly with the top of his foot. Time to show them how he'd earned the nickname. Time to take charge. He struck the ball hard across field, but it was over-hit. It skidded off the greasy turf and ran harmlessly out of play.

'Oh, for crying out loud,' moaned Ant. 'I'd slipped my marker then. All I needed was a half-decent ball.'

Kev held up his hands. 'Sorry.'

Anything half-decent seemed beyond him that Sunday morning. Just when he thought he'd left his past behind him, Jelly Wobble and co had to happen. Like a plague of boils.

'Sorry?' grumbled Ant. 'Sorry doesn't win matches.'

To Kev's relief nothing had come of the Blessed

Hearts' attack and Jimmy Mintoe was already bringing the ball out of defence. Kev found himself admiring the close control. Jimmy was a natural wing-back, good in the tackle but quick and creative on the break. He was some dribbler too. It was as if the ball was superglued to his boot. Licking boys Kev's new team might be, but they weren't without a bit of flair. It was a puzzle really. What *were* they doing limping along so badly at the bottom of the table?

'Jimmy,' he cried, slipping behind two flat-footed opponents. 'Come on, cross it.'

He could see it all, two of the Blessed Hearts' defenders pulled out of position, their full-back returning from an attacking run and nobody else in sight. One burst of acceleration and he would have the goal at his mercy. Then he heard Bobby Jones' voice booming from the touch-line. 'You've had your instructions, son. Back into position.'

Kev hesitated. Jimmy was already steadying himself for the cross.

'But . . .'

'You heard me. Back. I'm not having us caught on the break.'

Kev pulled up in disbelief but not before Jimmy had flighted a sweet cross-field pass right into his path. Without anyone running on to it, it was a gift to the nearest Blessed Hearts' centre-back. Kev winced as Jimmy started cursing him loudly for slowing up.

'So what happened to you this time?' Jimmy demanded angrily.

'Ask Bobby. Called me back, didn't he?'

Jimmy raised his eyes. 'Take no notice of him. He's a spare part, if ever there was one.'

Spare part or not, Bobby was the manager and he

looked the sort who would drop anyone who tried to stand up to him.

'Kevin,' shouted Bobby. 'Behind you.'

Kev spun round in time to see the Blessed Hearts' skipper taking the ball in his stride and setting off down the left.

Luke Costello, he thought, another old enemy.

'Well, don't just stand there. That's your man. Get into him.'

Kev powered after Costello, but he was already away. Before Kev could make up any ground Costello had hit a cross from the touch-line. It wasn't particularly well-directed and nobody was quite sure if it was a shot or a cross, but the way things were going it didn't matter. It dropped sickeningly over Joey Bannen's flailing arms and into the net. Four-nil down and it wasn't even half-time.

'This your Terminator, Jamie?' John O'Hara asked sarcastically. ' "Guv's boss," you said. "Fierce tackler," you said. "Takes no prisoners," you said. So how come two of their goals are down to him? Some Guv'nor.'

'Give him a chance, John,' said Jamie. 'It's only his first game for us. He doesn't even know all the lads yet.'

'It'll be his last,' John snorted irritably. 'If this is how he plays.'

'Behave,' said Jamie. 'We were on a losing streak well before Guv arrived. And we all know who that's down to.' He glanced towards the manager pacing out the touch-line. 'Five defeats on the run and he wasn't playing in any of those.'

John wasn't listening. He had said his piece and was stamping away, shaking his head.

'It's all right,' said Jamie. 'He's a right moaner. He had to have a go at somebody.'

'No,' said Kev. 'It's true. I've let you down.'

'Forget it. Just play yourself into the match. Hello, here we go again.'

'Push up,' Bobby was shouting. 'You're giving them too much possession, and how's about some service for Gordon?'

'What's the point?' Jamie muttered under his breath. 'He's wasted every ball we've given him.'

The back of Kev's neck was burning. He knew Blessed Hearts were laughing at him. Long, needling hyena guffaws that got him right in the pit of the stomach. They'd got their hooks into him and they were twisting the barb. What he wouldn't give for a miraculous come-back.

'Come on, lads,' Jamie urged, clapping his hands. 'Let's put them under a bit of pressure. This is embarrassing.' With that, he tapped the ball to Gordon from the spot.

'Gord,' shouted Dave Lafferty, peeling away to the left. 'Quick.'

But it wasn't in Gordon's character to release the ball. Kev had him sussed already. He was a glory merchant. He couldn't care less who was in space. Every time he got the ball he just made straight for goal. The Blessed Hearts' defence loved it. They were closing on him, ready to snap him up like hungry Rottweilers.

'Gordon,' Jamie barked. 'Pass it, will you?'

He didn't. Instead he ran straight into the biggest of the Blessed Hearts' centre-backs. It was suicidal – like charging a JCB head on.

'Oh, that was very intelligent,' groaned Dave Lafferty, looking down at a winded Gordon.

'Ever heard of team-work?'

'That's good coming from you,' snapped Bobby. He'd galloped anxiously on to the pitch the moment Gordon went down. 'You put him off with all your belly-aching.'

'I did what?'

'You heard.'

'Are you blind or stupid?' fumed Dave. 'You should be having a go at Superprat here, not me.'

Bobby's face went white with anger. 'That's the team captain you're talking about.'

'Yeah? Well the way I see it he couldn't skipper his way out of a paper bag! We're four–nil down and he hasn't even opened his gob yet.'

'Right,' said Bobby. 'I've had enough of your lip. Next time the ball goes out of play I'm taking you off.'

'Why wait?' said Dave, storming off the pitch. 'Here.' He peeled off his faded sky-blue shirt and flung it at Bobby. 'You can stick your team.'

The incident just about summed up the afternoon for the Dog and Gunners. Four–nil down and now Bobby had upset the only player who had given Blessed Hearts any trouble. Dave had actually hit the post when it was still nil–all.

'Aw Bobby,' moaned Jamie. 'Go after him. That was out of order.'

'You'll be off as well if you start arguing with me,' Bobby retorted. 'Who's the manager of this team, anyway?'

'Don't answer that,' Jimmy advised, tugging Jamie's shirt. 'Let's just try to get to half time without conceding another goal.'

Bobby didn't even get round to bringing on a sub. Ninety seconds later the ref blew, giving the Dog and Gunners a few minutes respite from the misery of another drubbing.

'Well,' Bobby demanded as the team flopped disconsolately to the ground to have their orange. 'And what do you call that?'

Nobody answered. The ten remaining players were still incensed over the row with Dave Lafferty. He had talent. He was a good laugh, too. Bobby, on the other hand, was about as popular as a dose of the flu.

'Well? I asked you a question.'

Still no reply.

'A shambles is what I'd call it,' Bobby informed them. 'Our defence had more holes than a colander.'

Jimmy and Ant gave him a furious glare. Who was he calling a colander?

'John and Jamie,' Bobby continued unperturbed. 'You were far too deep.'

Jamie rolled his eyes. 'I had to come deep,' he said. 'We couldn't get the ball off them.'

'As for you, Kevin,' Bobby went on. 'You've been about as much use as a glass buttock. How many times did I tell you before the kick-off? Man-to-man marking. Wherever that carrot top goes . . .'

'Costello,' Kev interrupted. 'His name's Luke Costello.'

'Whatever,' Bobby said dismissively. 'Wherever he goes, you go. He's taking us apart.'

'But I like going forward,' Kev protested. 'Remember when you pulled me back? I could have scored then.'

'And Barbie could keep goal for Everton,' Bobby answered, provoking derisive laughter. Some of the boys hadn't forgiven Kev his defensive errors. 'Now listen, we had a game plan and I want you to stick to it. We're playing four–four–three . . .'

'What?' Jamie interrupted. 'You want the goalie playing upfield?'

'You what?'

'Four–four–three. That makes eleven, twelve with the goalie.' Jamie gave the other lads a cheeky wink. 'Do you know a rule we don't?'

Kev was aware of a grey-haired man in a sheepskin coat a few yards away. He'd guessed he was one of the boys' dads. He was shaking his head at every word Bobby said. Bobby was obviously aware of him too, but doing his best not to rise to the silent criticism.

'All right, smart Alec,' said Bobby. 'Slip of the tongue. I meant four–four–two. Break down their attacks and hit it long out of defence. Gordon needs the ball if he's going to score. He's the only one playing.'

'Could've fooled me,' Kev whispered to Jamie. 'What planet's this feller living on? Gordon's a pudding.'

'Yes,' Jamie replied. 'But he's Bobby's pudding. Didn't you know? They're father and son.'

'Oh, so that's it.'

Jamie tapped his nose with his forefinger. 'That's all Bobby cares about. It's our Gord this and our Gord that. We'll be cleaning his boots if we don't watch it.'

'Yeah,' said Kev, inspecting Gordon's brand-new Predators. 'He thinks he's Gord Almighty.'

'Gord Almighty,' chuckled Jamie. 'I like that.'

Bobby didn't. He hadn't heard Kev's joke at the expense of his blue-eyed boy, but he didn't like laughter in the ranks. 'Settle down, lads,' he said. 'Now, Peter, I'm bringing you on in place of Dave.'

'Me?' asked a sallow, painfully-thin boy who'd spent the first half giving a running commentary on the game from behind the goal.

'Yes you, Ratso,' said Jimmy Mintoe. 'Do you know any other kids by the name of Peter in the team?'

'Ratso?' Kev asked Jamie.

'Pete Ratcliffe,' Jamie explained. 'Ratcliffe. Ratso.'

'Suits him,' said Kev. Mind you, polecat would have been just as appropriate. The lad was thin going on dead.

'Not half as much as Guv suits you when you're up for it,' said Jamie. 'What's happened to the aggression all of a sudden? You've been doing it for the school team. Why not for the Doggies?'

Kev's eyes were flicking nervously across at the Blessed Hearts' boys.

'I bet you could take this game by the scruff of the neck if you wanted,' Jamie continued.

Kev followed his friend on to the pitch for the second half. If he wanted! He would like nothing better than to lead his side storming back into the game, but how do you play when you're being reminded at every turn of the worst moment of your life? Remembering the hot July day when Mr Nolan suffered his heart attack. It was that that did for him, not the fire. Kev took a deep breath that shuddered through his chest. If only they'd let it rest. They didn't though.

'Burned any pensioners lately?' Jelly Wobble taunted as he trotted by.

Kev started. 'I didn't burn him,' he cried. 'You know that. It was an accident.'

'Yes, you accidentally set fire to his shed and accidentally gave him a heart attack.'

'And,' Luke Costello added, 'accidentally cleared off afterwards.'

'I never even knew he was there,' Kev protested. 'I never! We were just having a bit of fun. It got out of hand, that's all.'

'You know something?' said Jelly Wobble. 'You're pathetic. My dad says they should have locked you up and thrown away the key.'

'Kev,' Jamie hissed. 'Come away, will you? You're losing it.'

'Oh, he's losing it all right,' sneered Jelly Wobble. 'Losing you the match, and all.' He held up four fingers of his right hand and with the thumb and forefinger of his left he made a zero. It couldn't have hurt more if he'd branded it on Kev's skin.

'Like to tell us the score, McGovern?'

It was only a sharp blast of the referee's whistle that stopped the argument coming to a head.

'We'll have you, McGovern,' said Luke Costello by way of a parting shot. 'Just see if we don't.'

'Ignore them,' said Jamie. 'Let your feet do the talking.'

Kev had his chances to get into the game but each time he was tempted across the half-way line to pick up an inviting ball, there was Bobby waving him back into defence. The man in the sheepskin looked even more disgusted than he had at half-time. Kev was taking a liking to him.

'For crying out loud, Bob,' cried Kev. 'I always go forward. It's my natural game.'

'This is my team,' Bobby replied, 'So you do as I say.'

'Take no notice,' said Ant sympathetically. 'One decent crack at goal and he'll have to leave you alone.'

'You reckon?'

'I *know*.'

Kev felt encouraged. Moments later he was given the opportunity to shine. Costello had the ball, but he was getting cocky. He'd pushed it too far ahead as he took it into the Dog and Gunners' half. Kev was on him like a hawk, dispossessing him and punching a hole in the Hearts defence in one burst of acceleration.

'Run it, Kev,' shouted John O'Hara excitedly. His first-half grumbles were suddenly forgotten. Somewhere behind his back, Kev guessed that Bobby would be screaming his lungs out for him to stay in position, but he was away. His momentum had taken him to the edge of the Hearts' box.

'Kill him!' screamed Costello, stranded ten yards away.

Kev drove into the area and rounded the keeper. It was an open goal. He could almost hear the celebrations ringing in his ears. Don't swing at it, he told himself. Side-foot it. Accuracy not power. He picked his spot, then –

'Ref. Penalty, ref!'

Kev had been tackled from behind and crashed heavily to the ground. He was hurt, but it didn't matter. It would be his spot-kick, and no way was he going to miss. Not after the stick he'd taken from Costello and co. He was fired up. But where was the whistle? Kev rolled on to his side. The ball had bounced away and run free to Gord. Kev couldn't believe it; the ref was actually letting play go on.

'Trap it, Gord,' called Jamie. 'Plenty of time.'

He may as well have saved his breath. Gordon was doing a good impression of a disco-dancing giraffe. He swung at the ball and it spun away wildly, finally flattening the corner flag.

'At least he hit the woodwork,' gloated the Hearts' goalie.

'That was an open goal, Gord,' raged Jamie. 'An open flaming goal.'

'Yeah, you berk.'

'Space cadet!'

'A worm could have popped out of the ground and nodded that in,' groaned Ratso. 'Blindfold!'

'It should have been a penalty, anyway,' added John.

'That the best you can come up with, McGovern?' sneered Costello, as Blessed Hearts took the throw-in. 'Don't think you'll get another chance. We're going to bury you, lad.'

It was the last straw. Kev had had enough. 'Not if I bury you first.' He landed one on Costello. It wasn't a clean punch, more a smack on the neck and ear.

'Oh, want some, do you?' yelled Costello, shoving him in the chest.

'Come on then,' Kev blazed. 'Any time, Costello.'

But hostilities were interrupted by two short blasts from the ref's whistle. 'You two,' he roared. 'Cut it out.'

In an instant he was between them, doing that funny little quivery dance refs do when there's a punch-up on the pitch. 'Now that's enough. Any repetition and I'll have both your names. Now, play the game.'

Kev nodded, grateful for a second chance, and started to jog upfield, but Bobby was already trying to attract the ref's attention.

'It's all right, ref,' he said. 'I'm taking him off.'

Kev's muscles slackened in a gesture of defeat. He'd blown it, handed it to Blessed Hearts on a plate. Four weeks of being on his best behaviour down the drain. And any chance of glory with it. With the triumphant laughter of his opponents ringing in his ears, Kev trudged wretchedly off the field.

Two

'What's up, Kev? Picked up an injury?'

It was his cousin, Cheryl.

'No.'

'What then?'

Kev shrugged his shoulders. 'Where's your dad?'

'There, talking to your manager.'

As Kev looked across, his Uncle Dave detached himself from Bobby Jones. 'What's up, Kev? I thought we'd catch the whole of the second half. Not much point if you're not playing.'

Kev stared at the grass. 'I suppose not.'

'So what's the score?' asked Cheryl.

Kev mumbled the answer behind his hand.

'What?'

'Six–nil.'

'Winning?'

'Losing.'

'Six–nil? You're six–nil down?'

'That's right.'

'But nobody loses six–nil.'

'Looks like we do.'

'How did that happen?' asked Uncle Dave.

'See them big lads over there?' said Kevin. 'They just keep kicking the ball in our net.'

'Oh, very funny.'

'So why *are* you off?' asked Cheryl.

Kev gave her the evil eye. Trust her to bring it up again. 'He pulled me off.' He nodded in Bobby's direction.

'How come?'

Kev weighed up the chances of coming up with a plausible lie. Rogue iceberg, mistaken identity, mass hypnosis, sunspots. Then decided to tell the truth.

'I got involved in a bit of aggro, so he substituted me.'

Cheryl's eyes widened. It was one of her 'Not-again' looks.

Uncle Dave restricted himself to a simple observation. 'I thought you had more sense.'

'Well, he asked for it,' said Kev.

'They always do,' said Dave. 'But you don't have to give it to them. Bit of an Eric Cantona on the quiet, aren't you?'

Kev shrugged again. 'He was getting on my back. They all were.'

'Who are you playing anyway?' asked Cheryl. 'What team?'

'Blessed Hearts.'

'What, *the* Blessed Hearts? From where you used to live?'

Kev eyed Cheryl and Uncle Dave. That's torn it, he thought. I bet their minds are working overtime. It was a question of maths, really. Blessed Hearts+Kevin McGovern=World War III. Rumour had it the Kirkdale scallies could teach the Sicilians a thing or two when it came to vendettas. To Uncle Dave's credit, he didn't say a word.

'Want to go now?' he asked, changing the subject.

'Go where?'

'Back to yours. Your mum asked me to pick you up.'

Now it was Kev's mind that was working overtime. 'Why, what gives?'

'Oh, nothing in particular.'

That sealed it. It was like when the directors said they had 'full confidence in the manager' – meaning he was about to be sacked! Something was definitely up. Kev could always tell with Uncle Dave. The world's worst liar, he was.

'So are we making a move, Kev?'

'Can't I watch the end of the game?'

'Sure,' said Dave, furtively scanning the Jacob's Lane field. 'I'm in no hurry.'

Kev instinctively followed his uncle's gaze. There seemed to be a hint of anxiety in his roving eyes. He was definitely agitated. But there was nothing out of the ordinary. The usual six matches running simultaneously, that was all. Same as every Sunday morning in the South Sefton Junior League. Two thirty-minute halves with a size four ball. Twenty-two lads in each game, pitted against each other for a precious three points. Glory before your roasties for some, sackcloth and ashes with the pudding for others.

'I'm going to have another chat with this manager of yours,' said Uncle Dave. 'Be back in a minute.'

'OK,' said Kev the moment his uncle was out of earshot. 'Let's have it, Cheryl. Cough.'

'What do you mean?'

'What are you doing here?'

'Don't ask me,' said Cheryl. 'It was your mum's idea.

She asked my dad to pick you up.'

'I don't get it,' said Kev.

'What's there to get? She thought you could do with a lift home.'

'Don't be soft,' said Kev. 'She only fixes me up with a lift when she thinks I'm going to get into trouble.'

'Must add up to a lot of lifts,' said Cheryl off-handedly.

It was meant as a joke, but Kev didn't see the funny side. He gave her daggers.

'Sorry,' she murmured. 'That was a stupid thing to say.'

'I'm going to ask her when I get home.'

'She won't tell you,' said Cheryl. 'Not if it's important. Mine never do.' Her brow furrowed for a moment.

'All right, what is it?' asked Kev. 'What's on your mind?'

Cheryl indicated Jelly Wobble and Costello. 'Those lads, they keep staring. Do they know you?'

'What do you think?'

'And they know about the accident?'

'That's why I had to lay one on Costello,' said Kev. 'He wouldn't shut up about it.'

'And I thought all that was behind us,' said Cheryl.

Kev thought the *us* was a bit rich. Cheryl had never gone through hell. Not like him. She was all right though, even if she did like to shine her halo in public. She'd been a gem all through the trouble. You always knew whose side she was on.

'I thought it was over, too,' said Kev. 'Can't win, can I?'

They were interrupted by a loud cheer.

'Seven–nil,' said Kev. 'Come on, ref, blow the

whistle. Haven't we suffered enough?'

'You're not doing very well, are you?' asked Cheryl.

It was the understatement of the year.

'Five straight defeats,' Kev told her. 'Six with today's.'

'So you're bottom?'

'By a mile. Propping up the rest of the table. It was Jamie who asked me if I wanted to play. See that lad over there, Ant? He's Jamie's cousin, a founder member of the team.'

'There aren't many from our school, are there?'

'Me and Jamie, that's all. Most of them are from Our Lady's.'

Cheryl twisted her hair. 'So what did they want you for?'

'I've been doing all right in the school team. Jamie thought I might help give this lot a bit of backbone.'

'Didn't work, did it?'

Kev shook his head. 'Must have left my spine hanging in the wardrobe this morning.'

'You've really got into football again just lately, haven't you?' said Cheryl.

'Yes, I only let it drop when I started . . . Well, you know.'

'The fires.'

Kev looked away. It was a moment or two before he spoke. 'My mum was made up when I started playing again. She thinks it might keep me out of bother.'

'Will it?'

Kev gave her a level stare. She'd been a rock when nobody else would go near him, but he didn't think that gave her the right to nag at him.

'Tell you what,' said Uncle Dave, coming back up the pitch. 'That manager of yours is full of himself.'

'Noticed, have you? What did he say?'

'I just made the point that you don't win games if you don't attack. What's the point of a defensive formation when you're losing this heavily? Well, he jumped down my throat. After I'd done him a favour, too.'

Kev didn't get to ask about the favour. Uncle Dave's comments had attracted the attention of Sheepskin Man.

'Bobby Jones doesn't listen to anybody but himself,' he said. 'It's been like this all season. I'm Ronnie, by the way. Ronnie Mintoe.'

'Are you Jimmy's dad?' asked Kev.

'His uncle.'

'It must be Uncles' Day today,' said Uncle Dave. 'Kev here is my nephew. This is my daughter, Cheryl.'

'You were unlucky not to get that penalty, Kev,' said Ronnie. 'The ref should have blown the moment you went down. Stupid, playing advantage in a situation like that.'

'Yes, I know. I think we could have got into the game if we'd got a goal then. It was all downhill after that.'

'Bobby hasn't helped. You and young Davie Lafferty were showing a few touches until he took you off.'

'Thanks.'

'A bit of re-shuffling and these lads could make a good side. But they're going nowhere with Bobby Jones in charge. Uh-oh, corner.'

Luke Costello came in at the near post and headed another goal. It was a rout.

'I see what you mean.' said Uncle Dave. 'Is that seven?'

'Eight,' said Ronnie. 'Blow, ref. This could end up like a cricket score.'

In fact, it ended up nine–nil, with Joey toe-poking a goal-kick straight at Jelly Wobble. All the big lad had to do was knock it back. Joey came off with a face like a dripping tap.

'Goals don't come any softer than that,' said Ronnie as the final whistle went. 'See you. I'm going to get our Jimmy.'

'Yes, see you again,' said Uncle Dave. He turned to Kev. 'At least it didn't go into double figures.' It was his attempt at encouragement.

'Somehow, Dad,' Cheryl told him. 'I don't think you're helping.'

'Sorry, Kev,' said Uncle Dave. 'I didn't mean to make fun. I'm in a good mood, that's all.'

'Why, what's happened?'

'I've got a new job,' Uncle Dave announced proudly. 'Youth worker at the community centre on South Road.'

'What does that mean?'

'Trying to provide things to do for the kids on the Diamond. They certainly need something.'

The estate flashed through Kev's mind. Though he didn't usually give it much thought, he knew the Diamond had a reputation. It had its fair share of nicknames too: Fort Apache, the Twilight Zone, even Bosnia. There were all the usual things: mad dogs, mad kids, gangs, robbed cars, headcases careering round on motor-bikes, boarded-up houses covered in graffiti. It had its good points, though. Telling people you lived on the Diamond gave you a bit of kudos. Suddenly you were a roving ambassador for the Planet of the Ultra-Scallies, and somebody to be reckoned with. Lads thought twice before they mixed it with anyone from the Diamond.

'Walking back?' asked Jamie as he trailed off the pitch.

'No, my Uncle Dave's come to pick me up.'

'Jamie lives by our Kev,' Cheryl told her father. 'Why don't we give him a lift, too?'

'Sure, there's plenty of room,' said Uncle Dave. 'Oh, hang on, I need another word with your manager.'

Everybody looked puzzled.

'Right,' said Uncle Dave on his return. 'That's that sorted.'

'Like to tell us what's going on?' asked Kev.

'Bobby mentioned that he was short of somewhere to use for training sessions. I offered our community centre.'

'But I thought you didn't like Bobby.'

'I don't much,' Uncle Dave answered. 'Head the size of Birkenhead. No, I'm doing it for you lads.'

Five minutes later they were driving past the community centre. It wasn't much to look at, a squat blockhouse with chicken-mesh on the windows and a sign that read *So t R ad C mm ty C tr* because half the letters had fallen off. Sotrad Cummty Cutter, some wag had christened it; Sotrad for short.

'Bobby will be really grateful for this wreck,' said Kev sourly.

'I don't know,' said Jamie. 'It's better than what we've got at the moment.'

'Where's that?' asked Cheryl.

'Bobby's back yard.'

'You're kidding.'

'I am not. Ever tried passing practice when you've got to avoid the cucumber frame?'

'Can't say I have,' said Uncle Dave. 'But I can see why you lads are mad about your footy.'

'Why's that?' asked Kev. Might as well humour him. He was bound to tell them anyway.

'Well, just look around you. Not the sort of place for breeding brain surgeons or concert pianists, is it? All the great sportsmen came from the ghetto; Marciano, Muhammad Ali, Pele, Maradona, Dixie Dean, Georgie Best. Not many rich men in sport's hall of fame. Sport's a way out. It's either that or crime.'

Cheryl pulled a face. She hated it when her dad got on his soap-box. 'So how come you're always telling me to do my work at school and get a good job?' she asked pointedly.

'Yes, well there's that too, of course,' he answered half-heartedly. 'But there isn't much work on the Diamond, especially not for the lads. It's like I said, for half these kids it's sport or crime. You can tell who's going to go off the rails. They've got nothing, you see. No meaning to their lives. They just go on the rob.'

Kev frowned. It was all right for Dave to talk. He was the sort of guy who had never come off the rails, not really. All his life, Kev had been half-way off.

Just then Jamie nudged him. 'Look who's over there.'

'Who?'

'Brain Damage.'

'I can't . . . Oh yes, I see him.' He spotted Andy Ramage and Tez Cronin at the end of South Parade.

'You know what I don't get about Brain Damage,' said Jamie.

'What?'

'He messes about all day for Mr Hughes but whenever you see him, he's carrying his school bag.'

Kev chuckled. 'Whatever he's got in it, you can bet your bottom dollar it won't have anything to do with school.'

'Suppose not.'

Suddenly there was a loud crash. Tez and Brain Damage were lobbing half-bricks at the security shutters on the shops.

'What was that?' asked Uncle Dave.

'Just the two biggest scallies from our school,' Kev told him.

'What are they doing?'

'Bricking the shops.'

'What?'

Uncle Dave slammed on the brakes, throwing everybody forward. He unfastened his seat-belt and shoved open his door. Cheryl bit her lip. Oh no, not Mr Homewatch again. It wasn't the first time he'd taken after a gang of kids making a nuisance of themselves.

'Where are they?'

'You're too late,' said Kev. 'They legged it the moment you stopped the car.'

'They'd be better off down Jacob's Lane, kicking a ball about. Is this the sort of thing they usually get up to?'

Kev grimaced. 'What do you think?'

Uncle Dave gave a long sigh. 'I think they've just proved my point for me.'

Three

Cheryl had her ear to the door.

'Anything?' asked Kev.

'Sh.'

'Anything now?'

'No, they're keeping their voices down.'

'Move over. Maybe I can hear something.' But Kev had no more luck than Cheryl. 'What *are* they up to?'

There had been no Medusa stare from Mum when Kev walked in, so he had a feeling it couldn't be him they were discussing. For once.

'I want a video,' Gareth complained loudly. 'Mum said we could have a video.'

'Oh, button it, Pain,' said Kev. Brotherly love was in short supply that Sunday afternoon.

Gareth jumped up. 'I'm going to tell Mum on you.'

'There's no need for that,' said Cheryl soothingly. 'I'll put something on for you.'

'But he called me a pain.'

'So,' said Kevin. 'You are. Pain, pain, doughnut brain.'

Gareth immediately started wailing. Cheryl gave Kev a withering glare. 'Behave. What are you doing, arguing with a five-year-old?'

'I'm nearly six,' said Gareth.

'Nearly human, more like,' Kev grunted.

Gareth had his mouth open for another shriek of protest, but Cheryl got in first. 'Kevin!'

'All right, all right.' He held up his arms in mock surrender.

'Now,' said Cheryl. 'Which one do you want?'

'The one with the fish.'

'*Little Mermaid?*'

'No-o-o!' Gareth was offended. 'That's for girls.'

'He means *Jaws*,' yawned Kev. 'Duh duh, duh duh, duh duh, da, da, daaaa . . .'

'I don't.'

'What then?' Cheryl asked. She started waving videos at him, but Gareth shook his head at all of them.

'The one with the big nose and the cat and the fish in the bowl.'

'What?'

'He means *Pinocchio*,' said Kev.

'Right,' said Cheryl gratefully, '*Pinocchio* it is.'

She did her puppet walk and Gareth laughed. Kev stuck his fingers down his throat. While Gareth rolled on to his stomach to watch the film, Cheryl and Kev retreated to the sofa.

'I wonder where your dad is now,' she mused.

Kev sat bolt upright. 'What made you bring that up?'

'I don't know really. Mum mentioned him this morning.'

'She was talking about my dad? How come?'

'How should I know?'

'I bet she didn't have a good word to say.'

Cheryl screwed up her nose.

'They hate him.'

'Is it any wonder?'

Kev slumped back on the sofa. This could be the reason for the conflab in the kitchen. Something he hardly dared consider.

'What did your mum say?' asked Kev. 'Exactly.'

'Nothing much. Dad shut her up when he noticed me listening.'

'But what?'

Cheryl frowned. 'What do you think I am? A rotten tape recorder? I can't remember. Something like . . . Yes, I know. *You'd think he'd done enough to our Carol. It's about time she finished it.*'

'And that's what she said? Time to finish it.'

'Yes.'

Kev ran his hands through his black hair. 'So that's what she's after.'

'Are you going to let me in on this?' asked Cheryl.

'I think she wants a divorce.'

'It wouldn't make much difference, would it? I mean, you haven't heard a word from him in three years.'

'Of course it would make a difference,' cried Kev. The harshness in his voice made Gareth turn round.

'Watch the film,' said Cheryl gently.

'What's up with Kev?'

'Nothing.'

'Why's he shouting his head off?'

'Gareth love, just watch your film.' Cheryl waited for him to settle, then turned to Kev. 'He's a bit like me.'

'Who, Gareth?'

'No, Jiminy Cricket.'

Kev glanced at the top-hatted insect on the screen. 'You feeling all right?'

Cheryl laughed. 'I meant I could be your conscience.'

Kev scowled. It was the second time that day she'd reminded him what a Goody Two Shoes she was. You can only take so much sainthood in one person.

'I don't need a conscience,' said Kev. 'I just need a break. If she gets a divorce, that's it, he'll never come back.'

'You mean you still want him back?'

'Of course I do. He's my dad.'

'Not much of one. You've never even had a birthday card or a Christmas present from him.'

'So? Maybe he couldn't. Maybe she won't let him send them.'

'You don't think that, do you? If he'd tried to get in touch, I'm sure my mum would have told me.'

Kevin shook his head. 'Mum and Aunty Pat stick

— 29 —

together. They're twins, remember. Worst sort of Mafia you can get. They took a blood oath even before they were born.'

Cheryl considered the possibility of Tony McGovern out there somewhere, all sad and lonely and pining for his children. It was laughable.

'I wish I'd never mentioned your stupid dad,' she said.

'Well, you did.'

'You don't really expect him to come back though, do you?'

'Why not? Stranger things have happened.'

Cheryl shook her head. 'But he did so much . . .' She weighed her words, but there was no easy way of saying it. 'He was a villain.'

'What do you know? You're only repeating what your mum and dad tell you.'

'But he did things. You even saw him with your own eyes. You told me, remember.'

Kev's eyes flashed. Maybe he'd told her too much. 'What if I did? He's my dad, and that's all that matters.'

'You're living in a dream world, Kev. You're better off without him.'

Kev didn't stay around to listen to anymore. He was out of the door before she could take her foot out of her mouth.

'Oh, come back, Kev.'

As he thundered upstairs, Cheryl saw her Aunt Carol at the living-room door. 'What's up with our Kev?'

'I don't know.'

'I do,' said Uncle Dave from the kitchen. 'Pre-teen dementia. They all go through it.' He did his Whining

Teenager impression until Cheryl's mum hit him affectionately on the head with a rolled-up *Echo*.

'All?' asked Aunt Carol. 'Even Cheryl?'

'Even Cheryl. You should have seen what she was like over the trainers.'

'Oh Dad, they were gross.'

'What was wrong with them?'

'They were . . .' She paused as if struggling not to retch. 'Albanian. Whoever heard of Albanian trainers?'

'The lad on the stall at Paddy's Market for one.'

'They were disgusting,' said Cheryl. 'Drango's. Drango's Speclias.'

'Specials, you mean.'

'It said Speclias on the label.'

'Anybody can make a spelling mistake.'

'Adidas don't, Reebok don't . . .'

'OK, I get the message. I took them back, didn't I? Like I said, pre-teen dementia.'

Cheryl gave a thin smile. Whatever was wrong with Kev, it wasn't just pre-teen whatsisname. It went a lot deeper than that.

Four

I can't win, can I? I just can't flaming win.

Listen here, Kev, *they said.* Turn over a new leaf, *they said.* So I did. Keep your nose clean, *they said. Well, look at it. The cleanest rotten nose on Merseyside. I've been so good lately I'm expecting to sprout wings any day now. Get an interest, they said. So I've done that too. A lot of good it's done me. We got tanked in that match today. Worse than tanked – buried. We were a sick joke.*

There's me with my mind full of the Beautiful Game, the Golden Vision. And what are we really, a bunch of dead-beats, not worthy to scrape the mud off Duncan Ferguson's boots.

Then my mum drops her bombshell. She's binning you, Dad. OK, so maybe you deserve it, but she doesn't even ask me though, does she? No, I'm not even worth asking. Kev's just a waste of space, a good for nothing scally like his old man.

Gareth's the only one she ever has time for, the whinging little rat. He does all the right things, like colouring and making little cards that say: I love you, Mum. He's got more creeps than a rotten lizard. Why doesn't she take any notice of me?

Well, I'm going to show her, Dad. I am somebody. I am. I'm not going to let that team sink, and I'm not going to let them drag me down with them, either. We're going to have the club scouts sniffing round us like flies.

Everybody's been taking a pop at me long enough. Now it's my turn.

Five

'Oh, come on, Bob. Can't we do something else for a change?'

Bobby Jones waved away Jimmy Mintoe's protest. 'Fitness is what's letting you down. Now, twice round the field, and pick your knees up.'

'Fitness!' said Jimmy. 'Is he trying to say I couldn't outrun that fat kid on Sunday? Fitness isn't the problem. He's the problem. He must have learned his tactics from a lemming.'

Kevin pounded along beside him. Jamie and Ant were ahead of them and the rest of the boys were straggling along behind. Only there weren't that many of them. Kev took a head count: Jimmy, Joey, Ant, Mattie, John, Gordon, Jamie and Ratso. Eight plus himself. If the turn-out for the training session was anything to go by, they would be lucky to field a full side by Sunday.

'Pick up the pace,' shouted Bobby.

'Who does he think he is, a sergeant-major or something?'

'That,' said Jamie, 'is exactly what he thinks he is.'

Gordon looked a bit embarrassed. Kev was beginning to feel sorry for him. Maybe it wasn't his fault he was so selfish on the field. It was obviously his dad who was pulling the strings. You can't help your parents. It's not like buying a new pair of trainers. You're born with them, and if they're not up to scratch you can't just go out and get another pair. Worst luck!

'I said get your knees up!' bawled the sergeant-major.

'Why doesn't he get his own knees up?'

'Can't, his belly's in the way.'

They laughed, but only until a familiar voice broke up the party. 'Hey, Tez, look who's here.'

Kev's heart sank. Brain Damage. And there was that intriguing school bag lying on the ground at his feet. It was so out of character. Kev couldn't take his eyes off it.

'Well well,' said Tez Cronin. 'If it isn't the Guv'nor.'

'Get lost,' said Kev.

Tez and Brain Damage hooted their derision. 'Oh, don't be nasty to us, Kev baby. You'll hurt our feelings.'

'I said,' Kevin hissed, breaking off from the jogging group. 'Get lost.'

Brain Damage kicked the fence. 'What if we don't want to?'

'Then I'll have to come round and sort you out.'

They weren't impressed. They started kicking the link-chain fencing even harder.

'Oi, OI!' yelled Bobby, racing across. 'What do you think you're doing? This is council property.'

Wonderful, thought Kev, that'll really scare them. Two lads who'd smashed their own classroom window one evening weren't going to stop because of a jumped-up blurt like Bobby Jones.

'Shove off, Grandad.'

'Leave it, Bob, they'll get fed up.'

'You wish,' said Brain Damage. 'Who's Porky Pig here, anyway?'

'My name,' said Porky indignantly, 'Is Bobby Jones and I'm managing the team Kevin plays for. Now, why not go about your business and let us get on with our training session?'

If Bobby thought he was going to win Tez and Brain Damage over with sweet reason, he was in for a disappointment. They just loved winding people up. They stood on the other side of the wire, fingers pressed exaggeratedly to lips in mock innocence and eyes raised as if considering the request. 'Er, er, NO. If you want us to move *make us*.'

'Fair enough,' said Kev, making for the gate. 'I will.'

'Kevin!' barked Bobby. 'Come back here, now.'

Kev did as he was told, but not without a venomous glare at Brain Damage. Ever since he arrived on the Diamond, it had been hate at first sight. They had fights the way dogs have fleas.

'Look lads,' said Bobby. 'I don't know what your beef is, but we don't want any trouble. We just want to get on with our training.'

'If you don't want trouble,' said Brain Damage. 'What are you doing with Kevin McGovern?'

Kevin's heart turned over. Brain Damage knew things, and he was the sort to use them.

Bobby's face clouded. 'What do you mean?'

'Like what he did on Bonfire night. Ask him, why don't you?'

Kev's insides were twisting. 'Shut it, Brain Damage.'

'Why should I? You doctored our bonfire. You could have blown my head off.'

'I warned you about it, didn't I?' shouted Kev, a scream exploding inside his head. 'It was me that saved that ugly mug of yours. You were never in any danger.'

'Oh, that makes it all right, does it?'

'I didn't say that . . .'

Bobby had been listening intently to the exchange. He took Kev by the arm. 'Could I have a quiet word?'

Satisfied that he'd spoilt Kev's evening, Brain Damage aimed another kick at the fence then, bag in hand, he cycled away, followed by Tez.

'Like to tell me what that was all about?' asked Bobby.

'It was just a wind-up.' Kev was trying to sound calm, but the pulse-beat in his head nearly drowned Bobby's questions.

'Sounded a bit more than that to me.'

'It was nothing, honest. A prank.'

'Odd-sounding prank,' said Bobby, 'Look, I can't make you tell me, but I'm serving notice now. Any trouble and you're out of my team. I don't like your

attitude and I don't think your face fits. Put a foot
wrong and I'm chucking you out. Got that?'

Kev wanted to tell Bobby where to get off, but he
swallowed his pride. 'Got it.'

Jamie looked at Kev enquiringly. Kev just turned
away.

'OK lads, corner practice.'

There was a loud groan. What Bobby meant was
Set-it-up-for-Gordon practice.

'Joey in goal.'

'Aw, Bobby, you said you'd think about moving me.'

Bobby gave a cold smile. 'I've thought about it.'

'Yes?'

'And you're staying put.'

Joey kicked at the turf and dragged his heels for a few
moments before pulling on his gloves.

'Jimmy, Mattie, Anthony, John, you take up defensive positions. Kevin and Jamie, you knock a few
crosses over for Gordon.'

'What about me?' asked Ratso.

Bobby looked as if he'd been addressed by a cow pat.

'Oh, you mix it with the defence.'

'Right.' Ratso's voice changed. He was doing the
commentary off Sky Sports. He did it well, too. 'And
it's Liverpool's answer to Romario, diminutive goal-
poacher Ratso Ratcliffe buzzing like a hornet in the
box . . .'

Bobby pointed at him. 'And you can cut that rubbish
out, Peter.'

Bobby turned his back and Ratso used his hands to
make a gesture that said Big Belly – Double Chin.
Everybody laughed, even Gordon.

'Got something to say?' asked Bobby.

The team just stood there, suppressed laughter

swelling their cheeks as the manager's double chin wobbled indignantly.

'Then,' he said, 'we'll get on with it.'

Kev and Jamie knocked the balls in but Gordon didn't convert a single one. Either the defenders nodded the ball back out or Gordon missed altogether. He spent half his time untangling his studs from the goal net.

'Make your crosses more accurate,' said Bobby. 'How do you expect the lad to get them?'

'You what?' said Jamie. 'They've been inch perfect.'

'I think I know a good ball when I see one,' said Bobby.

'As Cinderella said to the Ugly Sisters,' quipped Ratso.

'I thought I told you to can it,' snapped Bobby.

'Lighten up, eh Bob,' said Jimmy. 'He's only having a laugh.'

'I'll lighten up when you lot start to play like you mean it.'

'But this isn't a proper practice,' said John.

'That's right,' said Joey. 'It's always the same. Run round the field then tee it up for Gordon. What about skills practice?'

'You need skills before you can practice them,' said Bobby caustically.

'Come on, Bob, that's not fair.'

'You're the ones doing all the complaining,' said Bobby. 'Let's have it, then. What's the gripe?'

'Obvious, isn't it?' said Jimmy. 'We keep getting thrashed.'

'Yes, and there's no game plan,' said Ant.

Joey saw his chance to raise his own grievance. 'I'm no goalie. You're playing me out of position.'

'Me too,' said Kev. 'You've got me in defence and I was top scorer in the team at my old school.'

'I know a lad who could keep goal instead of Joey,' added Mattie. 'Joey'd make a good full-back.'

Bobby held up his hands. 'Whoa, whoa. Slow down. I don't know what you're getting so hot under the collar about. It's only a game.'

That brought a chorus of hisses and catcalls down on his head. Like saying the Pope's just a vicar. Or the FA Cup's just a jug.

'All right, so what is it about?'

'It's about being a winner,' said Kev simply.

'That's right, Bob. We want to hold our heads up. You've had us all season and we haven't got a point yet. Not a flipping sausage.'

'Look,' said Bobby. 'I'm trying to make it work. That's why I've had you playing catenaccio.'

'Cat-a-what?'

'Catenaccio,' Bobby answered. He was gearing up for a history lesson.

'It's Italian,' Ratso interrupted. 'It means padlock, a defensive system perfected by the Inter Milan side of the mid to late sixties under coach Helenio Herrera. Only it proved vulnerable to the attacking full backs in the Glasgow Celtic team that beat them in 1967 to become the first British side to lift the European Cup.'

There was a stunned silence as everybody wondered whether Ratso had swallowed a football annual.

Then Jamie said: 'But I thought Man U were the first to win the European Cup.'

'The first *English* side,' said Ratso. 'Celtic, being Scottish were the first British side to become champions of Europe a year earlier.'

'Will somebody pull the plug on him?' asked an

exasperated – and slightly deflated – Bobby Jones. His thunder had been well and truly stolen.

'Sounds like he knows what he's talking about to me,' said Ant.

'That's right,' said Mattie. 'And what does *vulnerable* mean, anyway?'

'Oh, get a dictionary, lame brain.'

'I don't care if he thinks he's Bill flaming Shankly,' said Bobby. 'Let's get back to the subject in hand. I bet you don't even know what you want to change.'

'For a start,' said Jamie. 'You could listen when we tell you where we play best. Like Joey in goal. He's like a little garden gnome between the sticks.'

Joey blushed but nodded his agreement.

'Then there's the name,' said Ant. 'It sucks. I mean, Dog and Gunners, who wants to play for a side with a name like that? Sounds like we support the Arsenal.'

'Battersea Dogs' Home, more like,' said Jimmy.

'I thought it was quite clever, myself,' said Bobby.

'Clever?'

'Yes, it was the landlord at the Dog and Gun who raised the money for the kit.'

'And that's another thing,' said Jamie. 'What scouser would be seen dead in a sky-blue shirt? That's Man City's colours.'

'Don't forget Coventry,' said John.

'Now who could forget Coventry?' sneered Jamie dismissively.

'Besides,' Mattie added. 'It's all washed out. It looks a show.'

'OK,' said Bobby, 'So, besides the new kit, the new name and the new formation, what else do you want?'

'We could do with an anthem,' suggested Ratso.

Bobby shook his head.

'No, let him have his say,' said Kev. 'Go on, Rats.'

'Well, Everton come on to *Johnny Todd*. Man U have *Glory, Glory, Man United.* West Ham have got *I'm Forever Blowing Bubbles.*'

'That,' said Bobby, 'is the daftest thing I've heard yet. How are we supposed to play a theme tune?'

'I could bring my ghetto blaster,' said Ratso.

'This isn't a team,' said Bobby. 'It's a circus.'

'Who cares?' said Kev. 'So long as we win?'

'Look,' said Bobby, 'The name we can change. You just have to write in to the County FA. Any ideas?'

'How's about Norway?' said Jimmy.

'Norway?'

'Yes, like in the Eurovision Song Contest. Nul points.'

'Any *sensible* ideas?' asked Bobby. He waited a moment then continued. 'I'll consider changing the team around, too. But it's no go on the team kit, I'm afraid.'

'Why?'

'Do you know what a new kit would cost?'

'No.'

'About two hundred and fifty quid, that's all.'

The boys gave a low whistle.

'Looks like that's that,' said Ant.

'Why?' demanded Kev. 'We can't give up now. Look, we'll all bring suggestions for a new name to the next training session.'

'That's right,' said Jamie, 'And some ideas for fund-raising for a new kit.'

'Think we can do it?' asked Ratso.

'We've got to,' said Kev. 'Who wants to be a loser all their life?'

Six

'That you, Kev?' called his mother from the landing.

'No, it's the Incredible Hulk.'

'Why can't I ever get a straight answer?' she wondered aloud. 'I was getting worried. You're late.' She consulted her watch. 'Streuth, you *are* late.'

'Am I? We had a bit of a show-down with Bobby, that's all.'

His mother appeared at the top of the stairs, her hands shoved into the corners of a duvet cover. She looked worried. 'Show-down? There hasn't been any trouble, has there?'

'No, of course not. I mean we had a go at him over the team. It's going nowhere.'

'Oh, football,' she said with obvious relief. 'Is that all?'

'Why, what else would I be talking about? It was footy practice tonight, you know.'

'Yes, I suppose so.'

Kevin cocked his head. She was behaving oddly, distracted somehow. 'Something wrong, Mum?'

He couldn't disguise the little shake in his voice. The slightest change in her attitude and he expected the worst. Surely she couldn't have heard the stories Brain Damage was spreading about him? He still hadn't plucked up the courage to tell her the truth about Bonfire Night. Not the whole truth, anyway. How would he ever explain planting boxes of fireworks in somebody's bonfire?

'Wrong?' It was his mother's turn to sound anxious.

'There is, isn't there? What's happened?' He was startled by the sound of his own voice. It was excited, but scared. Then he knew what he had to do. There was never going to be a better time to ask her. He decided to pose the big question. 'Is it my dad?'

For a moment she just stood there, trailing the cover on the floor. All her defences were down. The look on her face unnerved him.

In a very small voice, he spoke to her. 'Mum?'

She glanced towards Gareth's room, then tossed the cover over the bannister. 'I'll be down in a minute, love,' she said.

Kev had been pacing the hallway for a couple of minutes when he realised he was still carrying his football kit around. He was on edge. He couldn't even sit down.

At last he worked out what his mother was doing. He could hear her reading Gareth his bedtime story. At a time like this? Couldn't it wait? Couldn't The Pain do something for himself just for once?

'Come on, Mum,' he hissed under his breath. 'Hurry up.'

But still she didn't come. Kev crept half-way upstairs, then, calling to mind something his gran said about watched kettles never boiling, retreated back to the hallway. Remembering his football kit, he picked it up and walked into the kitchen. It was while he was emptying it into the laundry basket that he heard her footsteps on the stairs.

'Well, is it him?' he demanded, meeting her at the kitchen door.

'Let's sit down, son,' she said quietly. Her voice sounded strange, remote somehow.

'Mum, tell me.'

'You're right, Kev. It is your dad.'

Kev almost choked on his own fear. It was true. The thing he had always dreaded. She was divorcing him. It was all over. Now they would never be a proper family again.

'He's back.'

Kev frowned. He heard the words, but they didn't make any sense. 'What?'

'Your dad. He's back in Liverpool.'

Kev stared across the table for a few moments, stunned.

'Did you hear what I said?' Mum asked.

This was something he had never expected. Maybe in the first few weeks after his father had left. But not for at least eighteen months. The idea of him coming back had ceased to be real. It had become a dream, like every Saturday evening when Mum sat in front of the telly clutching her lottery tickets.

'You've seen him?'

'No, your Aunty Pat did.'

'Where?'

'In the Strand. Pat couldn't believe her eyes. We think he's back at his mother's.'

Kevin searched inside himself for something to say, but he didn't know how to feel. It was crazy. All this time he had been waiting for news of his dad. Now that he finally had it came as a let-down. Dad was back, but not home.

'Is that why you were acting so funny on Sunday?'

She nodded. 'That's why I asked Dave to pick you up. Stupid, really. How would Tony know where you were? Even if he cared.' She paused for a moment. 'I know this is hard, Kev. I wasn't expecting it, either.'

Kev turned the matter over in his mind. Then

everything was clear. 'Why don't you go and see him? You could go now.'

'Don't be silly. It's late.'

'No, it isn't. Me and Gareth'll be OK on our own. Or you could ask Aunty Pat to come round while you're gone.'

His mother was struggling, like someone drowning. 'Kevin, stop it.'

'But he's so close. You could be round there in ten minutes.'

She ran her hand through her hair. 'I'm sorry, Kev. I don't want to, and I don't want you seeing him either.'

'But he's come back.' For us, he wanted to say, but he knew it would be too much for Mum to take.

'Kev, it's over between me and your dad. It was ages ago. I know you loved him, still do, but you can't expect me to let him walk back in here. Even if he wanted to.'

'But he's back,' Kev repeated. Nothing else mattered. Not that Dad had abandoned them, not that he'd done some bad things in his time. Just the one simple fact – he was back. Somehow it just wiped the slate clean.

'You're not listening, Kev. I won't be seeing your dad and neither will you. Not now, not ever. I forbid you to see him.'

Kev shoved back his chair. 'You can't do that.'

His mum was wavering between anger and tears. 'You don't understand.'

A ball of rage filled Kev's throat. 'That's not fair. Anyway, how are you going to stop me? I'm not little any more; I can go wherever I want.'

There was no mistaking the alarm in his mum's eyes.

Kev hated scaring her, but she had to listen to him. She had to let him see his dad.

'Kevin, this is crazy. You want us to play Happy Families, but it isn't like that. It never was. Please listen to me.'

'I won't listen. You just hate him and you want me to hate him. Well I won't.'

She reached towards him, but he pulled away from her.

'Leave me alone. You're spoiling everything. You want me to hate my dad, but I'll never do that.'

He stormed across the room. Slamming the kitchen door behind him, he shouted it once more at the top of his voice. 'Never!'

Seven

Back?

You can't be back. Not like this, anyhow. You were supposed to come back for us. Like in the films, a dark figure against the setting sun. There had to be a reason you walked out, something so big it was the answer to everything.

But you're back now, and you haven't come near. It's like I don't exist. You've come home, but not for me. I don't even matter. You've got things more important than me, haven't you? Anything's more important than me.

Three years I've been doing this, Dad. Three years I've been pouring my heart out. To you. But I made you up. I needed you. A proper dad, somebody who'd come back one day. Sometimes I really thought you were listening. No matter where you were. It always made sense, so long as I could believe there was something holding you back. But why don't you come, Dad? Tell me, eh? Aren't we even worth a visit?

Why don't you come?

Eight

'Something wrong, Guv?' asked Jamie.

Kev didn't answer. He just stared ahead at the late rush-hour traffic. The flyover acted as a magnet for kids from the Diamond. It was like something out of an Arnie Schwarzenegger movie, where the killer robots go around splattering the humans against graffiti-covered concrete walls. The flyover itself was dramatic enough, rising in an arc on huge pillars. That wasn't what drew the kids, though. It was the central reservation that ran underneath the flyover like a kind of concrete warren.

It was set below the road, with four pedestrian subways radiating from the heart of it. From the lowest point of the reservation rose steep banking, set with cobbles. What's more, the whole area was illuminated by powerful floodlights. Night or day, it was the place to hang out. Everybody used it for climbing or BMX stunts. The scallies smoked and spat and had fights.

Jamie tries again. 'Cat got your tongue?'

'What?'

Kev turned. They'd scrambled up the banking and were perched precariously on the barrier that separated the traffic from the central reservation. Their legs were dangling just inches from the speeding cars and lorries.

'I said,' Jamie shouted, assuming the traffic noise was

the problem. 'You look fed up. I thought you'd be on top form, what with your birthday coming up, and all.'

Kev's birthday hardly seemed to matter any more, but he wasn't prepared to tell Jamie why. Not this time. Some things are too much even for mates. The return of his dad was definitely one of them.

'I've been better.'

Jamie took the hint. There was something conclusive about the way Kev had said it.

'I like it here,' said Jamie.

'Me too,' Kevin answered. 'Especially at night.'

'Yes, I know what you mean. Like Mega City One, isn't it?'

They both looked up at the wintry evening sky. The inky blackness seemed to make the flyover even more massive.

'Think we can turn the team round?' asked Jamie.

'I hope so. We've got some good players. Mind you, we'd have had even better ones if Bobby didn't drive them away.'

'Dave Lafferty?'

'He was useful.'

'Yes, but you haven't heard the news yet, have you?'

'What's that?'

'Mattie's got us a new goalie. A proper one, somebody who actually wants to be in goal. Daz Kemble, his name is.'

'Where does Mattie know him from?'

'Dunno. Anyway, Mattie says he's a giant. Everybody thinks he's dead old. He could pass for fourteen or fifteen. It seems he dominates his area and yells at his defenders. Just like a real goalie. Bobby seemed impressed. He's got Daz to fill in a form. He can play this Sunday.'

'Can't be worse than Joey, can he?'

Jamie shook his head. 'It's not Joey's fault. He never wanted to keep goal anyway.'

'So why did he?'

'Why d'you think?'

'Bobby.'

'Got it in one. Gordon played in goal for the first game. Against Warbreck. He wasn't bad, either. Then he dropped the ball in front of one of their players and it ended up in the back of the net. Well, we gave him a bit of stick, didn't we? The trouble is, Gordon can't take it, so he's off whinging to his old man. The next thing you know we've got ourselves a new striker and there's little Joey in goal.'

Kev chuckled. He could just picture Joey sitting on the edge of a pond with a pixie hat and a rod.

'Tell me something, Jamie. Has the season been all bad? Haven't you even *looked* like winning?'

'Of course we have. We were playing this shower called Red House Rovers in the third game. Rock Bottom Rovers was more like it. Hammering them, we were. Three–nil up with twenty minutes to go and Bobby tells us to shut them out. It was stupid. We'd been all over them till then. It turned the game completely. Once we sat back and let them come at us, there were these huge holes opening up in our defence.'

'So what happened?' asked Kev. It didn't take a genius to know the story wasn't going to have a happy ending.

'We lost five–three. Everything went from bad to worse after that.'

'You know what we really need?' said Kev.

'What?'

'Somebody good on the wing. Somebody with a bit of real pace. John's pretty quick and Jimmy's good coming out of defence, but they both play on the right. We're dead predictable. Even when Bobby let us attack Blessed Hearts we were taking it through the middle all the time. Their defence just had to bunch in front of the box. We need to spread the play.'

'Sounds good, but where are we going to get a new wide player?'

Just then they heard a familiar voice.

'I don't believe it,' said Kev. 'Is he haunting me, or what?'

It was Brain Damage.

'What's he bawling at?' asked Jamie.

All they could see at first was Brain Damage cycling slowly around the central reservation, standing on his pedals. For once, he didn't have his mysterious bag with him. Unaware of the watchers at the top of the banking, he was peering into the subway tunnels.

'Come out, come out, wherever you are,' he called in a mocking, sing-song voice.

'I wonder what he's playing at?' mused Kevin.

'Nothing too innocent, I'll bet,' said Jamie.

Then, they saw Tez Cronin emerge from the tunnel that joined the reservation to the west side of the road. He held out his arms. 'I've lost him.'

'What about the others? Haven't they seen him?'

Tez shook his head. 'They've gone for a look round the back of the Baths.'

'We know you're here, Gooly,' called Brain Damage. 'We might go a bit easier on you if you come out now.'

The moment he heard *Gooly*, Kev knew exactly who they were after. You don't get too many families called Gulaid in the north end.

'It's Bashir,' he told Jamie.

'Yes, I'd worked that out for myself.'

Bashir was a Somali kid. His family had been living in Liverpool 8 until they were offered a bigger house on the Diamond. Funny kid, thought Kev. A bit of a runt and he had a weird accent, but he was about the only one apart from Cheryl who'd wanted to know Kev when the news of his trouble broke.

'Oh, stuff this for a lark,' said Brain Damage, dropping his bike to the floor. 'The lads are wasting their time looking around the Baths. There's only one place he can be.' With that he headed for the display of boulders in the middle of the reservation. 'You might as well come out,' he said. 'We'll find you anyway.'

Bashir didn't wait to be discovered. Breaking cover, he made for the nearest subway.

'Got him! Tez. Block him off.'

Even with the advantage of a bike, Tez was on to a loser. Bashir was small and squat, but he moved like a whippet and could twist and turn like an eel. It was as though he was on springs. Twice Tez made a grab for him. Twice Bashir jinked and shimmied and evaded capture.

'Shouldn't we give him a hand?' asked Jamie.

Kev nodded and steadied himself for the charge down the banking. Then something held him back. He took Jamie's arm. 'Hang on a minute. I'm not so sure he needs it.'

Brain Damage had jumped on to his bike and was pedalling furiously towards Bashir, but he'd reckoned without his victim's turn of speed.

'Tez, get out of the way!'

Bashir had slipped between them. Now there was nothing to stop them colliding.

'You soft get, Tez,' cursed Brain Damage, sprawling on top of his right hand man. 'I had him then.'

'Don't blame me,' said Tez, sliding a leg from under his spinning front wheel. 'You weren't looking where you were going.'

Meanwhile, Bashir had made his escape.

'Where'd he go?' asked Jamie, ignoring Brain Damage and Tez.

'Beats me,' said Kev. 'He's probably half-way home by now.'

'Couldn't he move though?' said Jamie, impressed.

'Not half,' said Kev. 'And I think he's left-footed.'

There was a pause. 'Guv,' said Jamie. 'Are you thinking what I'm thinking?'

Kev nodded. 'Let's just hope Bashir likes football.'

Nine

'Inter Walton?'

'No.'

'Real Walton?'

'No.'

'Borussia Waltongladbach.'

'NO!'

'Not Manchester United.'

'Too negative.'

'South Road FC.'

'Too boring.'

'The Beautiful South.'

'Been done.'

'Eh?'

'It's a pop group.'

'Oh.'

'The Sons of Dixie Dean.'

'No way,' Mattie Hughes snorted. 'I'm a Liverpudlian. I'm not having us named after some stupid Everton player.'

'Somebody who scores sixty goals in a season isn't stupid,' Ratso objected.

'So what *do* we call the team?' asked Joey.

'How should I know?' said Jamie.

Kev shook his head. 'This name business isn't as easy as I'd thought.'

'What about the fund-raising?' asked Jamie.

'Two pounds fifty,' said Jimmy Mintoe. 'Only the fifty p is an Irish one.'

'How did you get that?'

'Washing cars.'

'Where? In flipping Dublin?'

'Shut up, you. It took me all afternoon knocking on doors round ours. Everybody seems to use the car-wash all of a sudden.'

'Disgusting,' said Ratso. 'Next thing you know they'll be making Boy Scouts redundant.'

'Anybody else?'

'Seventy pence,' said John O'Hara. 'Selling old comics. It would have been ninety, but I bought this Judge Dredd off Ant's brother.'

'What about the sponsored silence, Ratso?' asked Mattie.

Ratso shook his head. 'I *owe* money on it,' he sighed.

Everybody laughed. Even with three pounds cadged from parents, the total kitty was uninspiring: six pounds seventy and the Irish fifty pence.

'Not bad,' said Ratso. 'Only two hundred and forty-three pounds and thirty pence to go.'

Ant tossed his shirt at Ratso. 'Just button it, will you? This is a disaster. We couldn't buy a set of studs for that.'

'It isn't a complete disaster,' said Ratso. 'I got the music.' He patted a carnivorous-looking ghetto-blaster, a portable CD that could start earthquakes. 'We'll psych out the opposition.'

But if anybody was psyched out, it wasn't Orrell Park Rangers. Bobby Jones' team-talk boiled down to this: They'd be playing Total Football.

'Eh?'

'You mean you haven't heard of Total Football?' asked Bobby.

'No.'

Bobby explained. 'Now do you see?'

'No.'

The lads didn't understand, and they knew Bobby didn't either. Then Ratso chipped in. 'Total Football was a system,' he informed everybody, 'in which players could take up any position and fill any role within a team's strategy. Dutch invention, it was.'

Double-Dutch was how it turned out for the beleaguered Dog and Gunners.

'This can't be right,' moaned Daz Kemble as he picked the ball out of the net for the second time in the first fifteen minutes.

'Of course it isn't right,' said Ratso. 'Everybody defends and everybody attacks, *but not all at once.*'

After a cavalry charge of an attack by the Dog and Gunners, Daz had been left without any defensive cover at all. Total Football was turning into a total disaster.

'Look,' said Kev, taking the ball to the centre circle.

'Let's get hold of this game, eh? We're running about like lunatics. Mattie and Joey, you two stay back all the time, OK?'

There were nods all round. The last thing anyone wanted was another 9–0 thrashing. Their pride just couldn't take it.

'We need to bring in our secret weapon,' said Kev. He was looking at Bashir who was hanging round uncomfortably. It wasn't an easy debut for the new boy.

Kev received the ball from the kick-off and looked up. Bashir had made himself free on the left.

'Bash.'

Kev punted a long ball out to him and set off down the middle to support him. Taking the ball on his instep, Bashir scampered down the wing.

'Look at him go,' shouted John O'Hara delightedly.

Bashir had left the full-back for dead and was in a perfect position to knock it in to the near post.

'Cross it, Bash,' shouted Jamie, making his run.

But Bashir had run out of steam. Swinging weakly at the ball, he let it trickle uselessly out of play.

'Never mind,' said Kev. 'Next time, eh?'

But the next time was exactly the same. And the time after that. All of Bashir's runs ended the same way. He could beat anybody for pace, but there was a problem with his final ball. There wasn't one!

'It could be worse,' said Jamie, as they trudged off at half-time.

'It could be better, too,' said Kev. 'If Bashir could get just half his crosses over, we'd be laughing.'

'What if somebody backs him up?' said Jamie. 'Does the crossing for him?'

'Who'd keep up with him?'

'They wouldn't need to,' explained Jamie. 'If they could even keep within passing distance, all Bash would have to do is roll it back. Then one of us could knock it in.'

'Sounds good to me,' said Kev. 'Let's talk to Bobby.'

As usual Bobby wasn't listening. He'd already taken the decision to bring off Bashir and put Carl Bain on in his place.

'Aw, give him a chance, Bob,' said Jimmy.

'Yes, he's dead quick,' said John O'Hara. 'I can't remember the last time we got behind anybody's defence.'

'Sorry, lads,' said Bobby. 'Bashir's off.'

'That's stupid,' said John.

'No,' said Kev. 'He's stupid.' He was looking straight at Bobby.

'What was that, Kevin McGovern?'

'You heard.'

'Right, you're off too.'

'You can't do that,' said Jamie.

'Why not?' demanded Bobby. 'I'm the manager.' Then, with venom, 'And he's a trouble-maker.'

'So what?' said Jamie. 'You still can't take him off. Carl's the only substitute who's turned up. We'd be down to ten men.'

Bobby scowled. Kev stayed on.

'What do you think you're playing at?' asked Jamie angrily as they took up their positions for the second half. 'Can't you control that temper of yours?'

'Well, he's getting on my nerves.'

'He gets on everybody's nerves,' said Jamie. 'But you don't catch us shouting the odds. Remember what happened to Dave Lafferty. Just keep a lid on it, will you?'

Kev spotted Jimmy Mintoe's Uncle Ronnie watching. Sheepskin Man was shaking his head. As usual. And not at Kev.

In the absence of Bashir, Kev decided it was up to him to make the forays down the left. A natural right-footer, he found it impossible to cross the ball on the run. Instead, he had to check, switch feet and cross it almost like a free-kick. The break in his forward momentum usually gave Orrell Park time to get men back in numbers. As they tired, he did begin to have some luck, though. One time, Kev's marker lost his footing, but Gordon put it over the bar. Another time, he turned his man inside out and cracked it in low. Again, Gordon couldn't even hit the target.

'For crying out loud, Gord,' yelled Kev after the third cross he had blazed wide. 'That was a sitter.'

'Leave him alone,' Bobby ordered from the line. 'He's playing like two men.'

'Yes, both thick and useless,' Kev retorted.

Short of a substitute, Bobby could only fume from the sidelines. Meanwhile, untroubled by the Dog and Gunners strike force, Orrell Park held on for a two–nil victory.

'Now I know what a turkey feels like,' muttered Jamie as they left the field.

'Yes,' said Kev, 'Stuffed for Christmas.'

Ten

'Lost again, eh?'

Kev stopped in his tracks. Brain Damage was leaning against a lamp-post outside the community centre, his bag swinging at his side. For once, he seemed to be on his own.

'On Sunday,' Brain Damage continued. 'I hear you lost again.'

'What's it to you?' growled Kev.

'Nothing, I just wondered if you were making a habit of it.' He nodded in the direction of Kev's team-mates leaving the practice session. 'I'll tell you something for free. It'll need more than training to get that shower winning.'

'Do us both a favour,' Kev snarled. 'Say it again. Go on, give me an excuse to spread you all over the pavement.'

Brain Damage just smirked. 'I hear Gooly's playing for you now. You must be hard up.'

Kev hated even having to listen to Brain Damage. It made him feel dirty. Up until then he'd hardly even wondered how Bashir felt about the aggravation.

'Have you been spying on us?' asked Kev. He glanced behind. Bashir was walking towards them with Jamie and Ant. Kev wanted Brain Damage out of his hair before they arrived.

Brain Damage ignored the question. 'They don't play though, do they? Not their game.'

'You stupid, or what?' snapped Kev. 'What about Stan Collymore, Les Ferdinand, Andy Cole. . . ?'

'British blacks,' retorted Brain Damage. 'I'm talking about the likes of Gooly here, the Afros . . .'

Kev's throat was dry. Even if Bashir had been a complete moron he would have defended him against Brain Damage and his foul mouth. But Bash wasn't; he was becoming a mate.

'You know something, Brain Damage?' Kev hissed. 'Your nickname suits you down to the ground. I've known brighter slugs. No African players, eh? What about George Weah, Tony Yeboah, Finidi, Amokachi, Ndlovu? All African, all flaming brilliant. You know what you want to do: open your mind and shut your mouth.'

Brain Damage just came bouncing back. 'Forgotten you're white, have you?' he asked.

'Listen you,' said Kev, twisting his strong fingers in the fabric of Brain Damage's Timberland top. 'You make me puke. When you open your mouth it's like taking the lid off a sewer. Bashir's my mate, so shut it. Now do one before I really lose my temper.'

Brain Damage didn't even flinch. His blue eyes stared right into Kev's and he really hit Kev where it hurt. 'Don't get so uptight,' he said. 'I thought you'd have been made up that your dad's back.'

Kev stiffened. 'How do you know about that?'

'Heard it. Off our Lee.'

'And how does your Lee know?'

Brain Damage laughed. 'He should do. He's given your old feller a job.'

'Don't be soft.'

'Have it your way, but it's true.'

Kev looked at Brain Damage. He didn't give much away.

'That's right, big buddies your dad and our Lee. Like that they are.' He crossed two fingers to emphasise their closeness.

'You're making it up.'

Kev's heart turned over. Lee Ramage was a complete headbanger. The whole street knew it when he came round to visit his mother at 70, Owen Avenue. He drew up in this flash BMW with the windows wound down and the CD blasting. But nobody ever complained about the music. Under Lee Ramage's silk suits there was a street fighter. One who meant business. A few years ago he'd moved from the little family terrace on the Diamond out to one of the posher parts of West Derby. But he still came back to visit. Nobody asked where he got the money to afford West Derby.

'That's right,' said Brain Damage, enjoying Kev's discomfort. 'Your dad and our kid are in the same line of work.'

'I didn't know your Lee was a boxer.'

Kev winced as the words came out. They made him sound like a right divvy. He knew exactly what Brain Damage meant. Boxing wasn't Lee Ramage's game.

'A boxer? That's a laugh. No, and neither is your dad. Not any more, anyway. It runs in the family, doesn't it? You're all losers.'

Kev ground his teeth. It hurt to remember that night three and a half years ago. His mum had taken a phone call. Dad's manager ringing from Gateshead. He'd taken a hammering from some Geordie and he was in hospital. The image was there in his mind, like an open wound. It was as real as if he'd witnessed the whole thing himself. His dad laid out unconscious on the canvas. And standing above him, the sweating victor, arms raised in triumph and grinning from ear to ear. It had been the end of Dad's boxing career. In less than two months he was gone.

Kev made as if to turn away. 'You're making all this up.'

'Am I? What if I told you your old man was round ours the other night—'

'Round yours!' Kev couldn't believe his ears. His father could visit the house of his worst enemy, not ten doors away on Owen Avenue, but he couldn't even call on his own family.

'After he'd gone, I started asking about him, so Lee gave me this stuff. Makes interesting reading, doesn't it?'

Brain Damage produced a bag of sweets and started munching nonchalantly. 'Oh yeah, he's big-hearted, our Lee. He'll even take on a bum like your dad . . .'

That did it. Kev grabbed Brain Damage's mouth and forced it open. 'See this mouth of yours?' he shrieked, the pain and humiliation boiling inside him. 'I'm going to close it for you.'

Brain Damage twisted and struggled, but there was no breaking Kev's grip. His muscles drew tight and the resistance stopped. Pushing his face right up to Brain Damage's, Kev snarled his contempt. 'You're a liar, Brain Damage. You don't know a thing about my dad.'

'Ask him yourself,' mumbled Brain Damage through his twisted lips, 'You go to your old man and ask him.'

'I don't need to,' said Kev, icy fear stealing through him. 'You're a stinking liar.' He wrenched the bag of sweets out of Brain Damage's hand and rammed it between his teeth. 'There, I hope you choke on them.'

'You're sick, McGovern,' yelled Brain Damage, as he retreated down South Road. 'You know that? You think you're something special, but you're nothing. Just an animal. A mad dog, that's what you are.'

By then, Kev's mates had caught up.

'Now what?' asked Jamie. Kev gave him a sideways look. It could have been Cheryl asking.

'Nothing I can't handle.'

'You shouldn't let Damage get to you,' said Bashir. 'Just ignore him. He wants you to react. It's stupid. I have to put up with a lot more than you do.'

'Easier said than done,' murmured Kev. 'And you should hear the way he talks about you. I couldn't just take it the way you do. I don't know how you do it.'

'I haven't got much choice,' said Bashir. 'I've been on the run from the likes of Brain Damage much of my life.' A grin lit up his usually expressionless face. 'That's why I'm so quick.'

'Quiet now, boys,' warned Ant. 'Here comes Bobby. Don't let on there's been any aggro. He'll flip.'

'Goodnight, lads,' said Bobby walking to the car with Gordon. Then, in almost the same breath. 'Oh, I don't believe it!'

'What's up, Bob?'

'Something wrong?'

'Only my car, that's all. Look, they've nicked the hub caps. That's over a hundred quid's worth.'

'They've been at the door lock, Dad,' said Gordon. 'Look, the radio's gone.'

'And look at this; they've even robbed my badges.'

Kev looked at the oval spaces where the Ford badges had been.

Bobby slung his Adidas bag on the pavement in temper. 'Just look what they've done to my paintwork,' he raged. 'Who'd do a trick like that?'

The boys did their best to look sympathetic.

'I ask you,' he went on. 'Who?'

Kev felt Bobby's eyes on him. Accusing. 'It wasn't me!'

Bobby didn't say another word. He just tossed his bag in the boot and climbed into the driving seat.

As the blue Scorpio pulled away, Jamie nudged Kev. 'So who do you think did it?'

Kev eyed Brain Damage, still visible in the distance. 'I wonder.'

Eleven

Well, have you got any more surprises in store? Oh, that was a stroke of genius, wasn't it?

You had the whole of Liverpool to pick from, but you have to get yourself mixed up with the Ramages. I don't suppose you'd know that Brain Damage is my worst enemy, but you wouldn't care anyway.

I ask you. Just when I thought I had him sorted. Just when I thought he couldn't hurt me, you show up and cut the ground from under me. Oh, it can't be true, can it? Not Lee Ramage. Imagine what Bobby Jones will do with this. He's got enough of a downer on me as it is, what with the car break-in and all. He hasn't half got it in for me. What have you got to hang around with Ramage for?

I mean, we're here. Just a few doors away. Is it that much effort to come and see us? It's your family that matters, not Lee Ramage and his druggy mates.

What a great birthday surprise, Dad. That's right, eleven in case you'd forgotten. I've had to grow up without you, but I've done it. Didn't have much choice. I've still got your boxing medals. That's right. They're in that old suitcase we took to Butlin's. I've got it hidden under my train set. It's pathetic but that holiday we had was the best week ever. Remember we went on the chair lift and went hunting crabs in the rock pools on that little beach? Mum was stuck changing Gareth's nappy, so it was just you and me. No scams, no disappearing acts. I mattered. We were a real family then. So what's so hard about that? Why can't you just do it. There are other kids in our class whose parents have split up, but their dads still come to see them.

*They take them places, have them over at weekends. But
you've got to be different. Why can't you play the game?*

*Please, Dad, remember my party tomorrow. Give it a
go, even if it's just for one day.*

Twelve

Kev flew to the door the moment the bell went, but it
was only Uncle Dave coming back from turning off his
car alarm.

'I'll have to get it seen to,' he said. 'It went off at four
o'clock in the morning last week. I'll be dead popular
with the neighbours.'

Kev did his best to hide his disappointment, and
returned to the party.

'I know who you're expecting,' said Cheryl. 'But he
won't come.'

'How do you know?'

'Stands to reason, doesn't it? He's missed your last
three birthdays. What makes you think he'll turn up to
this one?'

Kev knew that Cheryl was right, but he hated her for
it. He didn't care what made sense. It was more the
way things ought to be that mattered to him, and a dad
ought to be at his son's eleventh birthday party.

'Hey, Guv,' shouted Jamie from the far side of the
room. 'Heard what Ant's just told us?'

'No, what?' He was glad to disengage himself from
Cheryl. The last thing he wanted to do was to let slip
his dad's involvement with the Ramages.

'Only that Dave Lafferty's thinking of playing for
Blessed Hearts.'

'Get away.'

'Yes, they approached him after our game with them.'

'Can't blame him,' said Ant. 'Not after what Bobby did.'

'He could show some loyalty, though,' said Jamie.

'That's right,' said Ratso. 'We'll look a bit sick if he helps them beat us sometime.'

'Can't be helped,' said Kev. 'We'll just have to get along without him.'

'Pity, though,' said Jamie. 'He was good.'

'So are we.'

'Really?' said Ant. 'Were you at a different game on Sunday?'

'What I mean,' Kev replied, 'is we could be good. We've got skilful enough players.'

'So what?' said John O'Hara, joining the conversation. 'We've also got Bobby Jones.'

'Yes,' said Ratso. 'The Junior League's answer to Graham Taylor. The manager from Hell.'

'I'll tell you what,' said John. 'Either we pick up, or I'm looking for a new team, just like Dave.'

'You wouldn't.'

'Watch me.'

The announcement hung like a cloud over the others.

'Anybody come up with an idea for a name yet?' asked Jamie, trying to change the subject.

'I've thought of one,' said Ratso brightly. 'Queen of the South. Get it? South Road. Queen of the South.'

'Behave,' said Ant.

'Yes, the Dog and Gunners is better than that.'

'Sorry for breathing.'

'It's no wonder we're not winning,' said Kev. 'Look

at us. No kit – not a decent one anyway – a manager who hasn't got a clue, and, to cap it all, no name.'

'I've got it!' cried Ratso.

'Go on.'

'The Team With No Name.'

He was met with sullen glares.

'You mean I haven't got it?'

'NO!'

Before Ratso could come up with another suggestion, Kev's mum was rapping on the table with a spoon.

'Can I have everybody's attention for a minute?' she said. 'Come here, Kev.'

Kev gave her his most long-suffering Mu-um look. 'Come on.'

'That's right, Kev,' said Uncle Dave. 'Speech!'

Mum laughed. 'Don't embarrass the lad. Listen, Kev, I hope you've had a good birthday. You probably think you've had all your presents.'

Kev felt very self-conscious, standing there in his brand-new Everton shirt.

'But I've got you one more,' Mum continued. 'The last few weeks you've made me proud of you again, Kev, and I know it hasn't been easy. It's taken effort, and courage. What I'm saying is, you've come through, son.'

She gave him a hug and handed him a box, the sort that holds a pen or a necklace. It was neither; it was a watch.

'Turn it over, Kev,' his mother urged.

There was an inscription. *For you, Kev.* Then the words she had just used: *You came through.*

'Thanks, Mum.'

'That's all right, Kev,' she said. 'You deserve it.'

'Let's have a butchers,' said Jamie later, as they hung around outside the house after tea. He gave a low whistle. 'It looks a good one. I bet it set her back a few quid.'

Kev pulled his wrist away. He didn't like the mention of money. He knew his mum went short to get him and Gareth things. Suddenly he was feeling bad for shouting at her after training.

'Fancy a kick-around?' asked Ant.

'Yes, why not?' said John. 'My dad will be round to pick me up in half an hour.'

The front door was open and Kev could hear raucous laughter. Uncle Dave had brought a few six-packs and Kev's party had given way to one for the adults.

'Let's leave them to it,' said Kevin. 'We'll go down the garages at the end of the Avenue.'

The garages were meant for the tenants, but the cars had been burned and vandalised so often that nobody used them. A couple still had their locks intact, but the rest were completely gutted. It was as good a place as anywhere for a game of football. There was only one draw-back; the pensioners whose houses backed on to the garages used to grumble.

'Coming, Bash?' asked Kev.

'I don't know,' Bashir said uncertainly.

'Why, what's up? A bit too near to Brain Damage's house?'

Bashir nodded.

'Don't worry about him,' said Kev. 'You're with the Crazy Gang. He wouldn't dare try anything, not even if all his mates were with him.'

'Mind if we tag along?' asked Cheryl, coming out of the house. She had Helen in tow.

'Oh, they're not playing, are they?' moaned Jamie.

'You're not, are you?' asked Kev anxiously.

'Never heard of girls' football?' asked Helen.

'Yes,' said Ant. 'But this ain't it.'

'You don't really want a game, do you?' asked Kev pleadingly.

'If I say no,' Helen teased. 'Then you owe me one.'

Kev winced. It looked like she still had her stupid crush on him.

'Why don't we listen to Ratso's music instead?' said Cheryl.

So off they went to the *thump thump thump* of some Chicago rap-artist, eight boys, two girls and a ghetto-blaster. Kev liked it, knocking round in a gang. He enjoyed the wary looks of the passers-by and the twitch of the pensioners' curtains. He was part of something, a street scally. Most of all, he liked knowing Brain Damage wouldn't dare try anything.

'I thought it was a good suggestion,' said Ratso, kicking the ball against the garage doors.

'What's wrong with it anyway, the Team With No Name?'

'Team with no points, more like,' said Jamie.

'Yes, led by the manager with no brain,' said Kev.

'And no car badges, either,' said Ant. 'You reckon it was Brain Damage who nicked them?'

'Who else?' said Kev, slamming the ball against a fence. 'He was the only one hanging round.'

Jamie nodded, 'And his Lee deals in knock-off. My dad told me.'

'That's not all he's into,' said Ant darkly.

The mention of Lee Ramage made Kev's ears prick up, but nobody noticed. Jamie simply went on with the story. 'I reckon he gets Brain Damage and his mates to do a lot of the robbing and he sells the stuff on.' He jogged after the ball. 'Hey, watch this.' He trapped the ball.

'Go on, then,' said Cheryl. 'Impress us.'

Jamie struck down on the side of the ball with his foot. It spun up in the air. In mid-flight he caught it with his knee and tapped it up on to his head.

'Good, eh?'

Cheryl smiled. 'Not bad.'

'You want tricks?' said Kev. 'Give it here.' He held the ball between his ankles, bent both knees then jumped into the air bringing his ankles up behind him. As he flicked the ball into the air, he swivelled and volleyed it as it dropped. Unfortunately, it cannoned straight into the window of one of the bungalows.

'Oops,' said Helen.

'Hey, clear off!' An old man had stuck his head out of the window. 'Can't you read?' He was pointing to a sign. 'No ball games allowed,' he read, only paint balloons had been thrown at it so that the No was covered up.

'You listening? Clear off.'

'What do you think?' Jamie said. 'Should we move?'

'Better had,' said Kev. 'My mum will only ground me if he goes round to ours complaining.'

'Sorry, mate,' called Ratso.

'Don't you mate me,' the man retorted. 'Sling your hook. Young hooligans.'

'You know something,' said Kev thoughtfully as they wandered back towards Owen Avenue.

'What?'

'If that was Brain Damage nicking Bobby's stuff, he might still have it on him.'

'So?'

'So that's him over there.'

Sure enough, Andy Ramage was sitting on the kerb with his trusty bag. Tez Cronin and another lad were peering inside.

'Are you game?' Kev asked the others.

'I'm in,' said Jamie. 'I'm dying to know what he's got in that bag.'

'Yes, me too,' said Ant.

'Leave me out,' said Bashir.

'Well done, Bash,' said Cheryl. 'It's nice to see somebody with a bit of sense.'

'Oh, that's not it,' said Bashir. 'He'd only get me back later, when none of you are around.'

'Well,' said Kev. 'What are we waiting for? Let's get him.'

By the time he was alerted by the sound of trainer soles on the pavement it was too late for Brain Damage.

'Leg it!' he cried, but Kev and Jamie were already on him.

'Do one,' Kev ordered Brain Damage's mates. 'It's this moron we want.'

'Get off!' screeched Brain Damage. 'Let go of me.'

'We will,' said Kev. 'Just as soon as you let us have the stuff you robbed from Bobby Jones.'

'What stuff?'

'His trim,' said Jamie. 'And his badges. We know it was you.'

'That all?' said Brain Damage, surprising them all with his lack of concern. 'Here. Take what you want.' He dipped into the sports bag.

'Look at this lot,' said Ant. There were two car radios, a fog lamp, some window wipers and a pile of badges. 'There must be twenty here at least.'

'Twenty-three,' said Brain Damage. He wasn't one bit bothered that he'd been caught.

'You robbing get,' said Kev.

'What're you going to do about it?' Brain Damage demanded. 'Shop me?'

Kev saw the knowing look in the other boy's eyes. As if it was reminding him who his dad was tied in with. 'You know we can't do that,' Kev answered. 'We just want Bobby's stuff back.'

'You've had it with the hub caps,' said Brain Damage. 'And the radio. I've flogged them already. You can take these though. They're not worth anything anyway.'

Ant tossed Bobby's badges to Kev then returned the bag to Brain Damage.

Suddenly, Tez Cronin who was standing across the road waiting for Brain Damage yelled out. 'Police car!'

A patrol car had pulled up. The driver stayed inside, but the other officer got out and walked towards them. 'What have you got there, kids?' he asked.

Brain Damage reacted violently, thrusting his bag into Kev's hands and making a break for it.

'Hey!' The policeman started to follow Brain Damage, then thought better of it. Kev just stood there, paralysed by the turn of events. It was like a waking dream. Or nightmare.

'Right, son,' said the policeman, 'Let's take a look.'

Thirteen

'Have you had a good day, Kev?'

Pushing to the back of his mind the menacing

thoughts that had haunted him all the way home, Kev smiled at his mum. 'Yes, brilliant. Thanks for the watch.'

He meant, thanks for the inscription.

'I'm pleased you enjoyed yourself,' she said, clearing the table of plates and paper napkins. 'Kev.'

'Yes, Mum?'

'You're happy, aren't you?'

He knew immediately what she was getting at, but this was a conversation he didn't need. He might just give something away.

'How do you mean?'

'You, me and Gareth. We're a family, aren't we?'

Kev tied the bin-bag of party leftovers and headed for the bin. 'Of course we are.'

Out in the back yard he took a deep breath. There were snow-flakes in the air and the evening sky was a deep purple. It went without saying, didn't it? They were a family. The best. He loved his mum. But even the best isn't everything. His dad was out there, less than a mile down the road.

Who knows, he could be just a few doors away at that very moment.

'Don't stay out there long,' Mum called. 'It's bitter.'

Kev stared out across the waste ground behind the back fence and wondered what his dad had been doing all those years, where he had been. Most of all, why he'd never so much as sent a birthday card.

'Kevin, how long does it take to put a bin-bag out?'

Kev went back inside.

'I think you know what I was asking,' Mum began, as he leaned against the kitchen units. 'You still want to see your dad, don't you?'

Kev nodded. It was as much as he could manage.

'Has Kev got a dad?' asked Gareth suddenly. He'd been playing with his dinosaurs and neither of them had paid him much attention. 'I never knew that.'

'Of course he has,' said mum. 'The same one you've got.'

'*I* haven't got a dad,' Gareth answered bluntly.

'Don't be stupid,' said Kev. 'Of course you have.'

Gareth was getting upset. 'I haven't!'

Mum picked him up and sat with him on her knee. 'You have. It's just that you don't remember him. He doesn't live with us any more.'

Kev shook his head impatiently and started to walk out of the kitchen.

'Kev,' his mum said as he reached the door. 'Hang on a minute.'

'Why?'

'I thought we could talk.'

Kev nodded in the direction of Gareth who was tugging at her sweater. 'Talk to him instead.' As he walked upstairs he could feel the ache that must be filling his mum's heart.

Fourteen

So there I am standing there with this cheesey grin on my face and a bag full of stolen gear. A chip off the old block. It must have all happened in seconds, but it was like everything was in slow motion. There was this voice inside me saying: Give it up, Kev, they've got you banged to rights. Then there's this other voice and it's saying run for it. Just run. You've done nothing wrong. Don't carry the can for Brain Damage. Next thing you know I'm on my toes and this copper's shouting after me, but I don't stop. I daren't. It'd kill my mum. My heart's just banging like it's going to burst right through my chest. Then I hear Bash.

'In here,' he says.

So I'm in somebody's garden and Bashir's shoving me inside this dog kennel. A dog kennel, for crying out loud. I start shoving Bash back and telling him to get off. What if there's a Rottweiler in there?

Coppers or a Rottweiler, Bash asks, which do you prefer? And there I am, stinking of dog hair, with my knees wrapped round my neck. It did the trick; we lost the coppers. It scared me, mind. I had enough of that when I was setting the fires.

So why does everything seem to keep pushing me that way? Why?

I'll show them. Nobody's going to put me down any more. As far as I'm concerned, it's crunch time. It's make or break. I'm going to win this one.

You think I'm going to let Bobby go on telling me I'm rubbish? I'd eat glass before I'd let him slag me off again. It nearly got me in trouble with the law, getting his stupid badges back. But I've got them and I'm going to present them to him. I can't wait to see his face. A villain, am I? Well, I'm going to hand him his badges and wait for him to eat his words. Then I'm going to get the lads out on that pitch and show them what they can do. Forget the fancy tactics, all that cat-a-whatsit. It's going to be good honest graft. The boys are going to sweat blood if they have to. I won't be a loser and I'm not going to let them be losers. I'm going to sort it, me, Kev McGovern, and I don't need anybody else's help to do it.

Today's the day.

Fifteen

'Hey Bobby.'

'Oh, it's you, Kevin. You're late.'

Kev waved to Jimmy Mintoe and his Uncle Ronnie as he walked into the Jacob's Lane changing rooms.

'Heard the news, Guv?' asked Jimmy. 'Bobby's got Bash down as sub. I mean, he's seen the lad's speed. He's a real Andrei Kanchelskis. He could give him another chance, couldn't he?'

But Kev was hardly listening. He was dying to tell Bobby about recovering the badges. He felt quite the hero.

'Tell us in a minute,' he said. 'Well, Bob, don't you want to hear the good news? I've got a pressie for you.'

'Present? What sort of present?'

Bobby Jones' mind was on the game with Fix-It DIY. After seven consecutive defeats, he was even less disposed to listen to Kev than usual. Ignoring the frosty reception, Kev held out both fists.

'Which hand?'

'Look, Kevin, I'm in no mood for games.'

'Go on. Choose a hand.'

Bobby reluctantly tapped Kev's right fist.

'Ta da-a!' Kev announced with glee, opening his hand to reveal the stolen Ford badges.

'This some sort of confession?' asked Bobby sourly.

Kev's face fell flat. He'd been naive enough to expect thanks. 'What?'

'I hope you didn't take them.'

'For crying out loud, Bob. I got them back for you.'

'How?'

Kev lowered his eyes.

'Go on,' Bobby demanded. 'If you didn't nick them, then who did? Tell me. Who did you get them from?'

Kev was shifting his feet. It was one thing to challenge Brain Damage, even shove him round a bit to make him hand over over the gear. It was quite another to grass him up. Especially if doing it might end up leading to his dad.

'Come off it, Bob. I can't tell you that.'

'And why not?'

'You never tell on anybody, not even your worst enemy. It's the law of the land. You never spill your guts, not on the Diamond. Nobody does.'

Bobby took Kev by the elbow and drew him aside. Kev was aware of the inquisitive eyes of his team-mates turning in his direction. Ronnie in particular seemed to be taking an interest.

'So what about my hub caps?' asked Bobby. 'And the radio. They were worth something. The badges are buttons to buy.'

'I couldn't get the other stuff,' Kev admitted. He was beginning to regret trying to help Bobby.

'I'll make this short and sweet, Kevin McGovern,' Bobby continued, still holding on to Kev's arm. 'I never trusted you. Right from the beginning I knew you were trouble. I've got a nose for it.'

Kev pulled away. He could feel the injustice like a brand.

'Bobby?' asked Ronnie Mintoe. 'What's going on?'

Bobby ignored the interruption. 'Then there was that lad at the training session, the one who was kicking the fence.'

'You can't go believing Brain Damage!' cried Kev.

'He's . . .' But he couldn't go any further. That would mean doing the very thing he'd refused to do – grass him up.

'Oh, I'll bet he's a right young villain. You're cut from the same cloth, the pair of you. No, he just confirmed my suspicions, so I started asking around. I've been hearing things.'

'What things?'

'Fires for one thing. Tell me that isn't true.'

'I don't do it any more. Honest.'

'Then I heard something else.'

Suddenly Kev was wrong-footed. There wasn't anything else.

'That's right, somebody told me you were related to *the* McGoverns.'

Kev's heart kicked in his chest.

'Well, it's true, isn't it? Tony McGovern is your dad.'

Kev nodded wretchedly. Tears began to spill down his cheeks. There was no holding them back.

'Now stop right there,' said Ronnie who had come up behind Kev. 'That's well out of order. The boy's family is no business of yours.'

Bobby hesitated. He hadn't bargained for Sheepskin Man.

'I'm telling you,' Ronnie warned quietly, 'Stick to football, and leave the boy alone. Here, you almost forgot your badges.'

Bobby hesitated, then pocketed them. 'I don't think you quite understand, Mr Mintoe. I have a hunch Kevin might have been messing round my car. I've a good mind to go to the police.'

'You're wrong, Bobby,' said Ronnie. 'He was only trying to help.'

'That's your opinion,' said Bobby. 'It isn't mine.'

'You're not going to call the police, are you?' asked Kev anxiously. He could still see the policeman from the day before looking straight at him.

'No,' said Bobby. 'I couldn't prove anything, but if you make one wrong move, just one.' He paused for effect. '. . . Your feet won't even touch the floor. From here on in, I don't need much of an excuse to have you out of my team.'

With that, he walked away to start the team talk.

'You all right, Kev?' asked Ronnie.

'Yeah,' said Kev, wiping his eyes with his sleeve. Stupid get, he told himself. Fancy crying in front of a moron like Bobby Jones! 'Thanks for the back-up, Ronnie.'

'Forget it, Kev lad. Go and listen to the team talk.'

Kev nodded. He could hear Bobby going on about flat back fours and being quick on the break. 'For all the good it will do us.'

Ronnie smiled. 'Just play a blinder.'

'I'll give it a go.'

'Good lad.'

PART TWO

The Impossible Dream

One

'So what's the anthem this week?' asked Jamie.

Ratso was fiddling with the ghetto blaster. '*We are the champions*,' said Ratso. 'If I can get the rotten thing to work.'

'Why, what's up?'

A painful drone oozed from the speakers. The Fix-It DIY team started to laugh.

'What's that then, the funeral march?'

'I'm not surprised. They know what we're going to do to them.'

Ratso turned bright red. 'It's the batteries . . .'

The slow-motion dirge was getting even worse.

'They must be flat.'

'Tell you what,' called one of the Fix-It players. 'Those batteries are as flat as your form.'

'Hey,' added another. 'I've got the very song for you.' He started to sing tunelessly: *To dream the impossible dream.*

'Well done, Ratso,' grumbled John. 'That's a moral victory to them before we've even kicked a ball.'

'That's right,' said Ant. 'You and your stupid music. You're making us look right divvies.'

Kev watched the others take the field. Their heads were down before they started.

'Don't worry, Rats,' he said. 'It's not your fault.'

But Ratso was inconsolable. 'I should have checked the batteries,' he groaned. 'This sort of thing never happens at Goodison or Anfield.'

Kev tousled Ratso's hair. 'Come on, time to show

what we're made of.' He glanced fiercely across at Bobby. 'This is for pride, lad. For pride.'

Right from the kick-off Kev was on fire. He was determined to ram Bobby's suspicions down his throat the only way he knew how. He won three tackles in the first few minutes, breaking up every foray the opposition made into the Dog and Gunners' half.

'Come on, lads,' he shouted, clapping his hands. 'Stir yourselves. Start closing them down.' He saw some of the Fix-It players exchanging glances. This wasn't what they expected from bums propping up the table.

'Guv,' shouted Jamie. 'Your ball.'

Kev took up the pass and surged forward. He was aware of Bobby shouting instructions from the touch-line.

'Gord's free,' he was yelling. 'Cross it.'

Kev brushed off a half-hearted challenge and found himself on the edge of the penalty area. Gord was tussling with his marker, still trying to make himself available.

'Kev!' screamed Ant. 'To your right.'

Turning, Kev glimpsed Ant powering in. He'd left his marker for dead. Forget Gord, he told himself, the lad's a plank. Ant's the one. Take your time. Side-foot it. You've just got to roll it into his path. He closed his eyes. He actually closed his eyes and prayed.

'Goal. G-flaming-oal!'

It was mayhem. The whole team were after Ant, jumping on his back and grabbing his shirt. Ratso was going crazy, skipping in frantic circles, the usual Sky Sports commentary turning Brazilian. 'Magnifico, magnifico. Goooooooooaaaaal!'

'Kev's run,' panted Ant, disentangling himself from

— 82 —

the mob of players. 'Did you see it? Did you? Kev's run, Kev's pass.'

And that set off another chase, this time with Kev as the object of their adulation.

'Cut it out,' warned Kev. 'The first one who tries to kiss me gets knuckled. You'd think we'd scored at Wembley in the last minute. We've not won yet.'

'Yes, but we've never even been in front before,' cried Jamie. 'Don't you get it, Kev? We're actually in the lead!'

Confidence was running through the team like an electric charge. Even Bobby looked happy. He'd almost smothered Bashir when Ant's goal went in.

'Another reason not to be sub,' said John, jerking a thumb in their direction.

'Yeah,' Ratso. 'Imagine getting a hug off Bobby.' He started walking round doing pretend spits.

Everybody laughed. They were on a high. Too much of one, as it turned out. Fix-It came back at them straight from the kick-off.

'Don't go to sleep, lads,' yelled Kev. 'Jimmy, Mattie, close them down.'

But the attack had caught the Dog and Gunners defence napping. Even big Daz Kemble, who'd looked a safe pair of hands, was out of position. The movement of the Fix-It forwards left him stranded on the edge of the penalty area. The centre-forward looked up, glimpsed him out of position, and lobbed him. One–all.

'Typical,' bawled Bobby. 'Flaming typical. You get your nose in front and you let them straight back into the game.'

Ronnie Mintoe was standing next to him on the touchline. He tossed his head in despair. 'Bobby,' he groaned. 'Can't you even *try* to be positive? That doesn't help the lads.'

Bobby scowled and stalked away.

'Don't let your heads go down,' said Kev. 'Fight for every ball.'

Jamie and Ant nodded. At least they were up for it. Time after time it was the three of them who threw themselves into the tackle, breaking up the Fix-It attacks.

'I'll tell you what, Guv,' Jamie panted, after yet another sliding tackle. 'I'm shattered.'

'Nearly half-time,' Kev replied. 'Just keep it tight.' He nodded in the direction of a tall lad with sticky-out ears. 'And keep an eye on World Cup Head. He's good.'

Fix-It put together two more attacks but Ant cleared them both.

'That's it, Ant,' shouted Kev. 'Rock solid.'

Kev was in his element. Every time he praised somebody or urged them on he could see them growing. He had the gift. He was a motivator, a leader.

'Reckon we can win this, Guv?' asked Jimmy as he jogged up to take a throw-in.

'Why not?' asked Kev. 'No unforced errors, eh?'

Jimmy winked and threw to the only unmarked player. Bobby's blue-eyed. It was a bad choice. Gordon failed to trap it and it ran straight to World Cup Head.

'You balloon!' bawled Jimmy as Fix-It swept forward. 'Can't you even do that right?'

'Save the post-mortem for later,' shouted Kev. 'Get back in defence.'

They were chasing but Fix-It had caught them on the back foot. World Cup Head knocked the ball left, spreading the play. Kev saw the danger immediately.

While Joey and Ant raced for the winger, World Cup Head was running on into space.

'Ant!' Kev cried in panic. 'Don't get drawn out.'

It was too late. The winger cracked in a low drive that World Cup Head hammered in at the near post. They were two–one down.

'Oh, not again,' moaned John as the whistle went for half-time. 'I thought we'd turned the corner with Ant's goal.'

'Oh, quit moaning,' said Kev. 'We're only one adrift. I thought we had quite a good half.'

'Yes,' said Ant. 'Me too.'

Daz was walking past. 'You did well too, big guy,' said Jamie.

'Just wait for my party trick,' said Daz.

'What did he mean by that?' asked Kev.

'You'll see,' said Mattie Hughes. 'Wait for the last minute.'

'We didn't do much in attack, though,' said Jamie. 'Hey, Bob, what about letting Bash have another go?'

Bobby shook his head. 'Don't tell me how to run the team, Jamie. I'll tell you why we're losing. You're freezing Gordon out of the game.'

'Oh, put another record on,' said Jimmy.

'Watch your lip, son,' warned Bobby.

'But it's rubbish,' said Kev. 'Didn't you see how Fix-It got their second? They pulled us wide with that lad out on the wing. That's what Bash could do for us.'

'I'll do the team talk, thank you very much,' said Bobby. 'And since when did I appoint you captain?'

'How do you mean?'

'Don't come the innocent with me. I heard you, giving your orders. Gordon's the captain.'

'So why doesn't he say anything?' demanded Kev angrily.

'Maybe you don't give him chance,' retorted Bobby.

Kev threw himself back on the grass. 'Oh, I give up.'

'Get the ball to Gordon,' said Bobby. 'That's how to get back on terms.'

Even Gordon seemed embarrassed.

'That does it,' said John. 'I'm out of here.'

Bobby looked stunned.

'Well,' said John, 'What do you expect? You're going to lose us this one like all the others.'

'*I* lost them!' cried Bobby.

'As good as,' said Jamie, coming in on the side of John. 'Let us do it our way.'

Bobby looked at John hovering on the verge of departure. For once, he was lost for words.

'We're with Jamie,' said Jimmy, seizing on Bobby's indecision. 'It's Guv as captain or I'm off.'

'Me too,' said Joey.

Bobby looked livid, but faced with a mutiny he had to back down. 'OK, it's your funeral.'

'Well?' the boys asked, looking expectantly at Kev.

Kev bit his lip. What if he blew it? 'We bring on Bash,' he said. 'Yes, Bash for Carl. A straight swop. You don't mind, do you, Carl?'

Carl shook his head. 'No, I'm having a stinker anyway. Haven't been in the game.'

As the team took up their positions for the second half, Bashir edged over to Kev. 'I still can't cross it, you know.'

'Just run it, Bash. Then look for support.' He put on his ET voice. 'I'll be right here.'

Bashir nodded and ran off to the left.

If the Dog and Gunners were expecting a miraculous transformation, they were in for a disappointment. They weren't even given the chance to get Bashir away on the wing. From the moment he came on, they were under relentless pressure. First Joey cleared off the line, then Daz pulled off a couple of impressive saves.

'Nice one,' said Kev. 'So what's this secret of yours?'

'Just you wait and see,' said Daz. 'Wait for the last minute.'

'I don't think we can take much more,' said Ant breathlessly. 'They've got us on the run.'

'We've got to,' said Kev. 'If we can just see out the next few minutes we'll get our chance. They can't keep this up.'

But nobody had told that to Fix-It. They had the Dog and Gunners pinned in their own half. In less than a minute they hit the post and had the ball blocked on the line after a goalmouth scramble.

'Something's got to give,' said Daz as he sorted his defence for the resulting corner.

It did. Daz came for the outswinger and missed it completely. Kev challenged for the loose ball but World Cup Head beat him to it. Three–one.

'That's torn it.'

'Aw, Daz,' John complained. 'Why didn't you punch it?'

'I'll punch you,' snapped Daz.

'All right, all right,' said Kev. 'Don't start blaming each other. Let's just try to play ourselves back into the game.'

As he moved upfield he noticed Bobby.

'Look at him,' said Jamie. 'He *wants* us to lose. Just to prove him right.'

'Well,' said Kev, gritting his teeth. 'We're not going to lose. Are we, lads?'

Nobody answered.

'What's up with you?' he demanded. 'Lost your bottle? Well, have you?'

They were having doubts already.

Kev leaned over to Jamie. 'Take the kick-off. Give it to me.'

Jamie nodded. Taking the ball wide, Kev looked for Bashir.

'Bash,' he called. 'Yours.'

Bashir set off at a blistering pace.

'Bash, Bash,' yelled Kev, labouring after him, 'Back to me.'

But Bashir had outrun himself again. He tried to lay it back, but stumbled and let the ball run feebly to the keeper. Kev grimaced. He wasn't going to even risk a glance in Bobby's direction. He couldn't stand the flashing neon Told You So sign he knew he'd see.

'What now?' asked Jamie.

'More of the same,' said Kev. 'What else can we do?'

For a few minutes attack wasn't even an option. Fix-It came back strongly and were unlucky not to make it four–one.

'Just keep playing it to me and Bash,' said Kev, as the enquiring glances turned towards him. With less than ten minutes left he finally succeeded in putting Bashir clear. This time he went for broke, racing after the flying winger until he thought his lungs would burst. I'm still in touch, he told himself with amazement as he reached the penalty area shoulder to shoulder with his marker.

'Bash,' he screamed. 'My ball.'

Bashir looked across. He barely had to swing his foot

to roll it into Kev's path. Top of the foot, thought Kev. Hold off the defender with your body strength. Strike the middle of the ball, keep your foot firm. That's it, get over the ball and hit it.

'Goal!'

Kev could hardly believe his eyes, but there was the ball nestling in the back of the net. Three–two.

'Bash,' he gasped. 'We did it!'

He stood open-mouthed for a second then ran to fetch the ball. As he turned to race back to the centre circle, he started yelling. 'Come on, lads. We can win this. We've got them on the run.'

It was true. Fix-It began to panic and there was nobody on their side to steady them the way Kev had the Doggies. First Jamie seized on a poor pass and hit it over the bar. Then even Gordon got in on the act, heading narrowly past the upright.

'Corner, ref,' roared Kev. 'The keeper got a hand to it.' He knew he hadn't, but it was worth a shout. To Kev's utter astonishment the ref gave the corner. Even he seemed swept along by the Dog and Gunners onslaught.

'You cheeky beggar,' said Ant with a grin. 'That was no corner.'

'Sh,' said Kev. 'He'll hear you.'

And that's when he saw Daz.

'What the. . . ?'

'This is what I was telling you about,' said Daz, loping into the six-yard box. 'My party trick.'

Jimmy Mintoe took the corner, hitting a wicked inswinger. Kev started to go for it, but was suddenly aware of a green blur to his right. Daz in his keeper's jersey.

'Mine!' bawled the Dog and Gunners goalie.

Kev wasn't arguing, not with a runaway tree-trunk like Daz Kemble. Stepping aside, he left it.

There was a moment of confusion, then another moment of dead silence, then a shriek of joy.

'Goal!'

It was in the net. Three–all.

'We can win this!' shouted John, all his grumble suddenly forgotten in the joy of celebration. 'They're rocking on their heels.'

After that, the Dog and Gunners did their best to take the three points. Ant volleyed it inches over the bar and Kev went close again with a low drive, but time was the enemy. Before they could mount another attack the ref blew for full-time.

Two

'You have got to be joking, Bob!'

Alone among his team mates, Kevin had expected something like this.

'No,' said Bobby, 'I am not joking. I'm out of here. I've never been so insulted in all my born days. Come on, Gordon, we know when we're not wanted.'

Gord had a face like a week-old party balloon.

'But Dad . . .'

'Gordon, move yourself!'

Kev watched Bobby stalking away.

'Well, what do you make of that?' asked Joey.

Bobby had to almost force Gordon to the car. 'And don't expect me to come back,' he yelled as he bundled Jones junior into the passenger seat.

'Don't worry,' Jamie shouted back. 'We won't.'

'What a wally,' Jimmy observed.

'Good riddance to bad rubbish,' said Ant. 'Who needs him?'

'But who's going to run the team now?' asked John. 'If we don't have a manager, they'll chuck us out of the League.'

Suddenly faces were falling so quickly they had grass stains.

'Old misery's got something there,' said Jamie.

'Hey, Jimmy, what about your uncle?' Kev suggested.

'Do you think he'd do it?' asked Ratso.

'Only one way to find out,' said Jimmy.

The team watched as he jogged over to Ronnie Mintoe, who was looking on, bemused. A couple of minutes later Jimmy was dragging him over.

'This some sort of joke?' asked Ronnie.

'No way,' said Kev. 'Now that Bobby's thrown his hand in, we need a manager.'

'I'm no expert,' said Ronnie.

'And Bobby was?' said Ant. 'Let's face it, you couldn't do any worse.'

'Go on, Uncle Ron,' wheedled Jimmy. 'Give it a go, eh?'

Ronnie chuckled. 'After today, it looks like I'll be taking on a team on the up. Well, why not?'

The team gave a loud cheer.

'You'll take some licking into shape, though,' said Ronnie. 'You're a right bunch of rough diamonds.'

'That's it!' said Kev.

'What's what?'

'What Ronnie just said. Rough Diamonds. It's perfect.'

He confronted their puzzled looks. 'Do I have to

spell it out? We live on the roughest estate in the north end, and what's it called? The Diamond.'

'Yeah,' said Ratso appreciatively. 'The Rough Diamonds. Why didn't I think of that?'

'Cos you're a divvy,' said Jamie. 'That's why.'

'What about that Bobby, though,' said Jamie. 'Losing his cool like that? Next thing you know, he'll take his ball home with him.'

'Hang on,' said Ratso, looking around. 'He has, too.'

There was a moment's silence. Then everybody laughed. Like life was funny.

Three

'You're sure you don't mind, Carol?'

'Of course I don't mind. You'd do the same for me.'

Kev gave Cheryl a knowing grin as their mums went through the usual kid-dumping rituals. Final score. Three *Are you sure you don't minds* to Aunt Pat, against four *Don't worry about its* to his mum.

'I'll see you later then, love,' said Aunt Pat finally. 'I'll be up as soon as I finish work.'

Kev watched her slithering across the icy pavement to the car where Uncle Dave was revving impatiently.

'Come on, Pat,' he moaned. 'I've got to pick those presents up, remember.'

'What presents are those?' asked Kev.

Cheryl waved her parents off. 'Oh, Dad's arranging a party for the little ones down at the community centre. He's taking the presents there now.'

'What, and leaving them there?'

'Yes, they'll be locked up.'

Kev snorted. 'Since when did that stop anybody?'

'You always have to expect the worst, don't you?' Cheryl complained.

Kev didn't reply. 'A bit of luck about the school boiler, wasn't it?' he said. 'I wonder if we'll get another day off tomorrow.'

'I don't know about luck,' said Cheryl.

'Kev.' His mum was calling from inside the house. The front door was still open.

'Yes?'

'Are you and Cheryl going out?'

'Yes, I was going to call for Jamie.'

'Will you take our Gareth along with you? He's fed up of hanging round the house.'

'Aw, Mum.'

She appeared at the front door. 'Aw Mum nothing. I just want you to take him with you. Let him get some fresh air.'

Kev looked up at the flakes of snow swirling in the biting east wind. 'It's too cold for him. He's only little.'

'I'm big!' said Gareth.

'Yeah, for a midget.'

'I'm not a midgie!'

'That's just what you are,' said Kev. 'A moaning midgie.' Then in a sing-song voice: 'And you make more noise than a rotten budgie.'

'Mu-u-um!' wailed Gareth.

'He'll only start moaning,' complained Kev, pulling a face. 'Moan, moan, moan.'

'Not if he's rugged up warm,' said their mother. 'Now look after him.'

'*I'll* look after him, Aunt Carol,' said Cheryl. Kev really was making an effort to be good, but even a Making-the-effort Kev was still a handful.

'Thanks, love. Nice to see one of you knows how to act like an eleven-year-old.'

Kev scowled. 'Thanks a bunch, Cheryl. Now we're stuck with the Pain.'

Cheryl just shook her head and took Gareth's hand. 'So what are we going to do?'

'If this sticks we could have a snowball fight. Come on, we'll call on Jamie first. Oh, come *on*,' pleaded Kev, as Gareth stopped to gather the snow that was beginning to cover the garden walls.

'Be a bit more patient, will you?' Cheryl scolded. 'We'll get there soon enough.'

But when they did finally arrive at Jamie's, nobody was in.

'Jamie's out,' said Kev, glaring at Gareth. 'And it's all your fault.'

Cheryl jumped to her little cousin's defence. 'How do you work that out?'

'If he wasn't so slow, we'd have caught Jamie before he left.'

'Now you're being ridiculous.'

Gareth agreed emphatically.

'Hey, Kev,' said Cheryl.

Kev turned, and took a snowball full in the face.

'I'll get you for that!' he roared, bunching the powdery snow with his bare hands.

'No!' squealed Cheryl as he stuffed the snowball down the hood of her coat.

Gareth joined in on Cheryl's side and soon the three of them were giggling uncontrollably as they pelted one another.

'Hey, Guv,' came a shout behind them.

Kev turned, still smiling from the snow fight. 'Oh, it's you.'

Brain Damage was standing a few yards away with Tez Cronin and three other boys. 'Here,' he said, flinging his snowball.

Kev stood up defiantly and waited to be hit. But it wasn't just snow. Brain Damage had packed a stone inside. The moment it struck Kev there was a sickening crack and blood began to trickle down his temple.

'You pig, Andy!' cried Cheryl, inspecting the cut on Kev's face. 'That was a rotten trick.'

'I'll get you for that,' shouted Gareth fiercely, and ran at Brain Damage.

Brain Damage made no concessions for little kids; he just cuffed Gareth away. Kev immediately saw red. 'Don't you dare touch my brother, Brain Damage,' he yelled. 'Ever!' He flung himself at his enemy, but for once he'd bitten off more than he could chew. His mates closed ranks, and one of them swung at Kev.

'Look out!' warned Cheryl, glimpsing the flash of metal. 'He's carrying.'

Tez Cronin had produced a wheel brace and was swinging it at Kev's head.

'Let's get out of here,' Kev shouted. 'Run!'

Gareth did his best but fell to his knees on the snow-covered pavement. Kev scooped him up and led the flight down South Parade.

'Here,' said Kev, handing Gareth to Cheryl. 'Run into Sayers. Hang round the café till they've gone. You'll be safe. It's me they're after.'

'What about you?'

'What about me? Get inside, will you?'

The moment's delay was almost fatal. Kev's pursuers were on top of him, sending him crashing into the security shutters on South Road Off-Licence. Brain Damage managed to lay a hand on Kev's coat and Tez took another swing with the wheel brace, catching him a glancing blow on the shoulder.

'Kev!' screamed Cheryl. She turned, looking for passers-by. 'Help us, somebody!'

But Kev was quite capable of helping himself. He punched Tez in the chest, then tore Brain Damage's fingers off his coat.

'Just get Gareth home safely,' he panted, wrestling off a third attacker. 'Or Mum'll kill me.' With that he was off down the Parade with Brain Damage's gang snapping at his heels.

'Kev!'

'I want Kev,' said Gareth tearfully.

'I know,' said Cheryl, her voice full of confidence. 'He'll be all right.'

Inside she wasn't so certain.

'You're dead, McGovern,' yelled Brain Damage.

Kev heard the voice, but he wasn't about to reply. He'd gained the garages unseen. With any luck they'd carry on past.

'We've lost him.' It was Tez Cronin.

'No way,' said Brain Damage. 'He couldn't have had more than five yards on us when he turned the corner. He's here somewhere.'

Kev's heart was pounding as he crouched in the derelict garage. He didn't dare go any deeper into it for fear of being cornered, but here by the shattered doors he was hopelessly exposed. He thought of Bashir and his recent escape, but Kev had two big disadvantages. He didn't have Bashir's turn of speed, and Brain Damage had back-up. It was looking grim.

'Search the garages,' ordered Brain Damage. 'This

time I'm having him.' Then, with a raised voice: 'You hear me, McGovern? We're coming for you.'

Kev looked around frantically. Opposite him were the pensioners' bungalows. The fence wasn't too much of an obstacle, and if he could get through the gardens he might have a chance. He edged closer to the broken doors.

'There he is!'

Kev was face-to-face with one of the gang. Grabbing a scorched plank from the garage floor, he swung. His opponent ducked but it had done the trick. Kev was up and running before they could react.

'Get him!'

In four strides Kev was scrambling up the fence, scraping his wrists until the blood came, but scaling it before he could be caught.

'Go round,' shouted Brain Damage. 'Beat him to the front.'

Kev dropped to the ground then hurdled the small picket fences that separated the back gardens. He rattled an entry door. Locked. Backtracking, he tried another. It opened. He was on the street and heading back down South Road.

'Get after him!'

He could hear their footsteps, but he wasn't going to turn round. Keep your eyes on the prize, he told himself. Over the community centre fence, into Owen Avenue, home. The effort was burning his lungs. He was running on pure adrenalin. You've got to take it in one, he told himself as the community centre fence loomed. Don't look back, don't even think about them. Pace out the run up and straight over. He crashed on to the link fencing and forced himself up. Barely had he coiled his fingers round the line of barbed wire at the top than the whole thing started shaking.

'Pull him off,' shouted Brain Damage.

'That's right,' yelled Tez Cronin. 'Get him down.'

For a moment Kev's whole body swung free of the fence, hanging by his fingers, then he hoisted himself on to the top wire, avoiding the barbs. As he made to jump down, he gave a triumphant grin. But the celebrations were premature. The moment he launched himself he felt a jarring tug on his arm. He was snagged on something.

'Yes, we've got him.'

Kev saw Tez and another boy separating themselves from the rest of the gang. They were racing towards the front gate of the community centre grounds.

Another minute and he'd be trapped. He began to twist and wrench at the fence. Something snapped, but he gave a whoop of relief. He was free.

'Hey, Brain Damage,' he called defiantly. 'Drop dead!'

Then he was running again. He almost danced through the community centre gate, evading Tez and the other boy by no more than a yard.

'You know what, Tez?' he taunted as he pounded into Owen Avenue. 'You need to lose a few pounds of unsightly fat. Here's a tip for you; why not cut off that ugly head?'

All Tez could do was let loose a bellow of helpless rage.

As Kev closed the front door his whole body was shaking with triumphant laughter. And relief.

Four

'Where's my mum?' he whispered, as Cheryl ran to greet him.

'In the back, doing the washing. That cut looks nasty.'

Gareth grimaced. 'Ugh. Blood.'

Kev touched his head. 'It's nothing.'

Cheryl pursed her lips. 'It'll be nothing if Aunt Carol sees it like that. Get upstairs and keep out of sight. Where do you keep the cotton wool and TCP?'

'What? Oh, plasters and stuff. Kitchen drawer.'

While Cheryl went into the kitchen, Kev and Gareth sat on Kev's bed.

'You OK?' asked Kev.

'Yes. You hit the bad boys, didn't you?'

'Yeah. Well, I can't have them man-handling my little brother. That's my job.'

Gareth grinned. Kev was amazed. So the Pain had a sense of humour, after all.

'What's this?' asked Cheryl, walking into the room. 'Since when were you two such big mates?'

Kev shrugged. 'He might be a pain, but he's my pain.'

'Now,' said Cheryl. 'Hold still.'

She started dabbing at the cut on Kev's head.

'Ow!'

'Where on earth have you been?' asked Cheryl, inspecting Kev's arms. 'You're cut to shreds.'

'It's only scratches,' said Kev. 'So long as I wear long sleeves Mum won't notice.' Then he went pale.

'What's up?' asked Cheryl anxiously. 'Are you feeling sick?'

'Oh no,' breathed Kev.

'What?'

He held out his left wrist. 'My watch. The one Mum gave me for my birthday. It's gone.'

Five

Did the world ever cave in right on top of you?

It isn't the watch. It's because Mum gave it to me. She was saying thank you. Thanks for keeping out of trouble. What if she knew about that stolen gear? I came this close to breaking her heart, but I got away with it. I deserved that watch. I came through. I've got to do something. I just can't stand there and tell her it's gone. But what can I do?

Think, Kev lad. There's got to be a way out of this.

For once in my life, I'm actually starting to get somewhere. We were like giants in that last match. That's right. We had that Fix-It lot on the run. It's the first time we've got anything half right. I can't let something like the watch spoil it. I sorted the team, so I can sort a little thing like a watch. I just need to think. If I can just get over this then I'm on my way. I've got this feeling in my bones. These lads are special.

Six

'What's the time, Guv?'

'Half past twelve. Why?'

'My dad's taking me to Goodison this afternoon.'

Kev felt suddenly jealous of Jamie. Uncle Dave had treated him to a couple of Everton home games, but that was last season. Since mid-August he'd had to survive on Jamie's blow-by-blow accounts of the matches. Somehow, it wasn't much of a substitute for the passion of thirty thousand paying Scousers. Kev was a true Blue. Even truer and bluer than Jamie, but that didn't seem to count for anything. As usual, money talked and most weeks Kev's mum didn't have two pennies to rub together.

'You're proud of that watch, aren't you, Guv?'

Kev saw Cheryl giving him a warning look. Don't let on it's not the original. His voice faltered slightly. 'Yes.'

'It'll be your second visit of the day to Goodison,' said Cheryl's mate Helen.

'That's right,' said Jamie, 'And we'll be a step nearer the new kit.'

They were getting some funny looks, but they didn't care. So what if they were limping along Rice Lane with their ankles tied together with football scarves. Who cared how stupid they looked so long as the sponsorship money came in? A sponsored event had been Ronnie Mintoe's idea. But it had taken the special genius of Ratso Ratcliffe to come up with a three-legged limp from South Road to Anfield to Goodison and back. It was simple; three legs, three footballing venues.

'You didn't need to come,' said Jamie as he and Cheryl hobbled along arm-in-arm.

'Oh, we did, you know.' said Helen, giving Kev's waist a squeeze.

Kev winced. Helen still had this stupid crush on him and being tied to her with an Everton scarf would normally have been the ultimate nightmare. But it was Cheryl's price for bailing him out over the watch. She'd handed over the last of her birthday money to do it, too. When it came to saints, she was in the Premier League.

'Here we are,' said Jamie. 'South Road at last.'

'I can see John and Ant,' said Kev. 'And Ratso and Joey. We must be the last to arrive.' He had a feeling Helen had something to do with that. She didn't seem to want to walk to finish. At one amorous squeeze per lamp-post the replacement watch came at a high price.

'It doesn't matter, does it?' said Cheryl. 'We've raised the cash.'

As they entered the community centre gates, the rest of the team began to clap.

'Are we the last?' asked Kev. 'Where's Bash?'

Ant shrugged. 'Never turned up.'

'You're kidding?'

'Honest. We haven't seen hide nor hair of him.'

'Funny,' murmured Kev, then changing the subject: 'Do you know how much we've raised, Ron? Can we afford the new strip?'

'I've counted over a hundred,' answered Ronnie. 'But I've got a few more fund-raisers in mind.'

'Tell Guv the news,' said Ratso who was fairly rattling with excitement.

'What news?'

Ronnie smiled. 'Well, I know we'll raise the cash over the next few weeks so I'm going to advance the team the rest of the money. You'll be in your new kit by this time next week.'

'You're kidding,' said Kev. 'That's fantastic.'

'So what's it to be?' asked Ant. 'AC Milan?'

'Ajax Amsterdam,' suggested somebody else.

'No, somebody's got that strip.'

'Who?'

'Ajax Aintree, divvy. Who do you think?'

'Oh yeah, I forgot.'

'Real Madrid?'

'All white? Boring.'

'Behave yourselves,' said Kev. 'When it comes to footy strips, there's only one. Blue and gold.'

'Of course,' said Ratso. 'Pele, Juninho, Romario, Rivelino, Garrincha. The masters of the Beautiful Game.'

'What is he on about?' asked Mattie.

Ratso took a deep breath. Who was this Philistine? 'Brazil, of course.'

There was a collective sigh from the team. As Rolls-Royce is to cars. As the Koh-i-Noor is to diamonds. So are the Samba stars to football. 'Brazil.'

It was settled. In a week's time they would be playing in the blue and gold of the world's greatest footballing nation.

'You're made up, aren't you?' asked Cheryl, sidling up to Kev as he sat on his own to sip his Coke.

'Not half,' he said. 'By the way, thanks.' He held out the wrist sporting his replacement watch.

'It's a good job I knew where Aunt Carol bought the other one,' said Cheryl. 'Me and Mum helped choose it. Did you look for it?'

Kev nodded. 'I've been round the grounds with a fine tooth comb, but it's gone.'

Forget it,' said Cheryl. 'Just so long as your mum doesn't know you lost it.'

Kev inspected the watch. 'There's no way she could tell the difference, is there?'

Cheryl shook her head. 'Only if she picked it up and saw that there was no inscription on it.'

'I'll pay you back,' said Kev. 'Every penny.'

'I know you will,' said Cheryl with a smile. 'Look out. Here comes Helen again.'

'Oh, rescue me, for goodness sake.'

'Oh no,' said Cheryl, breezing away. 'That's the deal, remember. You be nice to Helen.'

Kev shook his head. 'The things I let myself in for.'

'Hi, Kev,' said Helen.

'Hi. Good grief!'

'What's up?' asked Helen.

Kev was staring right past her. 'It's Gord Almighty, and Bobby.'

Bobby and Gordon's entrance into the community centre had the same effect as the sheriff walking into a saloon in an old Western. You could have heard a cactus-needle drop.

'Hello, Bobby,' said Ronnie uneasily. 'What brings you here?'

'It's our Gordon. He still wants to play.'

'For us?'

Kev rolled his eyes.

'You must be joking!' said Jamie.

'No way,' said Ant.

'Now hang on a minute, boys,' said Ronnie. 'I think you should give him a chance. Not as a striker, though.'

'No,' said Jimmy. 'Stinker maybe, but not a striker.'

Gordon gave a lop-sided grin. He was choking on humble pie.

'I could try you elsewhere,' said Ronnie. 'No guarantees of a game, though.'

Bobby turned on his heel. 'Come on, Gordon,' he said. 'I know when we're not wanted.'

'Please, Dad,' said Gordon.

'What is this?' whispered Jamie. 'Gord standing up to his dad?'

Bobby hesitated.

'I want to play,' Gordon said.

'OK,' said Bobby. 'If it's really what you want. But I won't be hanging round to watch you.'

'Why don't you stay for a bit, Bob?' asked Ronnie. 'No hard feelings, eh?'

Bobby shook his head. 'No, we'll be getting off. We just wanted to ask about the team. By the way, how much did you raise today?'

Ratso held up the tin. 'Well over a hundred. We're going to count it properly after.'

'I'd be careful with that much hanging around,' said Bobby. He stared pointedly at Kev. 'You want to watch somebody doesn't take it.'

Kev started as if he'd had an electric shock. 'Why the—'

'Forget it, son,' said Ronnie. 'He didn't mean it.'

Kev shook his head. 'Would you like to put a bet on that?'

Seven

'Hi there, Bash,' Kev shouted, spotting the familiar figure wandering down Owen Avenue. 'We were expecting you on the sponsored walk today. What happened?'

Bashir's face told its own story. There was discolouring under his left eye.

'Who did that to you?' demanded Kev.

'Who do you think?'

'Brain Damage. I'll kill him.'

'Don't be stupid,' said Bashir. 'He's got all his mates with him. There's no sense us both getting done over.'

'Then I'll have him out on his own. One to one.'

Bashir shook his head. 'Since when did Brain Damage fight fair? This is my problem, not yours.'

'Give over, will you? We're mates.'

Bashir smiled. 'Yes?'

'Yes, of course we are.'

Kev felt guilty. Bashir had made all the running in their friendship, and Kev had never taken much notice. Bashir was in Year Five, so he'd always seemed too young to be a real mate. Too quiet, as well. Let's face it, he was too downright soft. Kev had been one to hang round with the scallies, courting trouble. It was, he'd always thought, what boys are for. Poor Bashir had seemed too much the underdog to be part of the Guv'nor's gang.

'So where did they get you, anyway?'

'By the garages. I was on my way to the community centre.'

'What did your mum and dad say when they saw that eye?'

'They haven't seen it. I haven't dared go home yet.'

'Why not?' asked Kev. 'It's not your fault you got battered.'

'That's not what I meant,' said Bashir.

'Then what?'

Bashir started to walk away. He seemed angry at Kev. 'You don't understand.'

'Then make me.'

'What if my dad goes round to Brain Damage's

house? The whole family will be on to him then. You know how they feel about us.'

Kev sat on the wall in front of his house. 'Oh.' He knew immediately that Bashir was right. The family had hardly been made welcome since they moved in, so complaining to the Ramages would only be inviting trouble.

Kev felt helpless. Taking it wasn't his way. For years he'd met every challenge with his fists. Or with fire.

'But it isn't fair,' he said.

'So?' said Bashir, giving him a pitying look. 'Who said it's meant to be?'

Kev sucked thoughtfully on his lower lip and stared at Brain Damage's house. 'People like him,' he murmured. 'They spoil everything.'

Bashir shrugged his shoulders. 'There's nothing you can do about them.'

'I should have shopped Brain Damage to Bobby. Yes, Cheryl's right. Maybe it is the answer, after all.'

'You'd never do that.'

'Why not?'

Bashir scratched the back of his head. 'I just know it'll never happen.'

As if to prove the point, a white BMW swung into Owen Avenue, sound system blasting.

'Talk of the devil,' said Kev. 'That's Lee Ramage now.'

They watched as the car drew up in front of number 70. Kev knew what to expect. The expensive suit, the close-cropped hair, the arrogant walk. But this time it wasn't Lee Ramage who attracted his attention. It was the man in the passenger seat.

'It can't be.' Kev watched the slim, muscular figure emerge. He was wearing a black bomber jacket and jeans. He glanced up and down the road then walked round to the driver's door and opened it.

'So it's true.' He stared in disbelief at the man scurrying round Lee Ramage. He was behaving like a servant, a lackey.

'Kev, what is it?' asked Bashir.

Lee Ramage and his minder walked quickly from the car and disappeared into the house.

'Kev?'

'That man,' Kev answered. 'He's my dad.'

Eight

I can't do this any more.

Three years I've been lying to myself. You know I actually thought you were worth it? You had to be. You just had to. I mean, whatever happened to happy endings? All this time I've been waiting for you, and look at you. Tell me this isn't happening. I've been waiting for my dad. Somebody to put things right. Fancy falling for that one. I must be one sad case. The kid who invents his dad. Pathetic. Just pathetic. But it's all up now. It isn't you, is it, that man who went fishing in the rock pools? That was a dream. Now I know what you really are. You're Lee Ramage. Or at least a carbon copy. Suck up to him if you want. Be like Lee Ramage if you want, but I'm not going to be like Brain Damage. No matter what it takes, no matter how hard it is, I won't end up like you.

Ever!

Nine

'Off, what do you mean off?'

'Off,' grumbled the Jacob's Lane groundsman, 'As in not on. Don't they teach you anything in that school?'

Kev pushed his way to the front of his disappointed team-mates to plead their case.

'Come on, mate. It's only a bit of snow. We're not wimps, you know.'

One of the Junior League committee members took the groundsman's fork and jabbed at the turf. 'See that, lads,' he said as the fork bounced off the frozen ground. 'You may think you're rock hard, but this ground's harder. We don't want any broken bones. The game is off. O-double F, off.' He gestured at the other teams making their way home. '*All* matches are off.'

'Yeah, yeah,' said Ant. 'We get the message.'

Ratso was looking sadly at his ghetto blaster.

'So what was today's theme?' asked Kev.

'*Simply the best*,' Ratso answered. 'I even got some new batteries to make sure the opposition could hear.'

'Simply the best,' came a sneering voice. 'You lot comedians, or what?'

'Who are you?' demanded Jimmy.

'I play for Longmoor Celtic,' said the newcomer. 'That's all you need to know. It's lucky for you it snowed. You'd have got battered.'

'No way,' said John. 'We're on a roll.'

'How do you work that out?'

'We drew our last game, that's how.'

'That's right,' said Kev. 'We've turned the corner.'

The debate had attracted a couple more of the Longmoor players. 'So how many points have you got so far?'

Suddenly none of the Diamonds were in a hurry to answer.

'Go on, how many?'

It was Daz who finally spoke up. 'One.'

'One point in eight games!'

It was a few moments before the mocking laughter subsided.

'Who did you get that against, anyway?'

'Fix-it DIY,' Joey answered defiantly.

'Fix-it? We gave them a good hiding. Seven–two.'

The Rough Diamonds exchanged glances. Suddenly, their three–all draw didn't look quite so heroic.

'Seven–two!'

The Diamonds watched the opposition walking away.

'Seven–two,' breathed John.

Kev could see the pride and confidence draining out of them. 'Listen to yourselves, will you?' he snapped. 'We started that game under Bobby, remember. Don't let those divvies psych you out. That draw was just the beginning.'

'You reckon?'

Kev tapped his temple. 'I *know* it. The moment you start thinking like a loser, you are one. I'll tell you this for free, I'm not having them walk all over me.'

'Guv's right,' said Jamie. 'We turned that game round at half-time. Imagine if we'd played that way from the start of the season. We'd be up there with the best.'

'I just hope you're right,' said John sceptically.

'I am,' said Kev.

As the team straggled back to Jacob's Lane, a car drew up.

'What's up, lads?' asked Kev's Uncle Dave. 'Match postponed?'

'That's right,' Kev replied. 'What are you doing here? Did my mum send you?'

'No, Ronnie did.'

'Ronnie?'

'Yes, he's working days and he couldn't get a swop, so he asked me to fill in for him.'

'What, like an assistant manager?' asked Jamie.

'Yes, I suppose so,' said Uncle Dave. 'Anyway, who wants a lift? I can take three of you.'

Kev glanced at his team mates. 'I'd better stick with the lads.'

'It's OK,' said Ant. 'You go.'

Kev and Jamie slid into the back. Cheryl gave them a smile from the passenger seat.

'Room for one more,' said Uncle Dave. 'Any takers?'

'Come on, Bash,' said Kev. 'Hop in.'

Bashir accepted the offer. He knew Kev was thinking about Brain Damage.

'So what does Ronnie do?' asked Jamie. 'I've never heard him talking about work.'

'No,' said Kev. 'Neither have I, come to think of it.'

'He's a fireman,' said Uncle Dave. 'Hayter Hill fire station.'

'A fireman,' said Kev thoughtfully.

It was a couple of minutes before anyone spoke. Nobody felt comfortable talking about fire with Kev around.

'Tell you what,' said Uncle Dave at last. 'Seeing as

you've got a couple of hours to spare, why not help me put labels on the presents for the Christmas party?'

'Presents!' said Jamie eagerly.

'Not for you,' said Cheryl. 'Unless you're into cuddlies. It's for the tots.'

'I'm game,' said Kev.

'Me too,' said Bashir.

'Go on,' said Jamie. 'Count me in.'

As the car crunched over the freshly-fallen snow covering the community centre car park, Jamie nudged Kev. 'Seen who's hanging round?'

'How could I miss him?'

Bashir followed their gaze and wrinkled his nose with distate. 'Brain Damage.'

'Well?'

Kev was doing his best not to look out of the window.

'Yes,' said Cheryl, flicking the blinds back in place. 'He's still there.'

'What's with you?' asked Jamie.

'What *is* the matter?' asked Cheryl as Jamie went to help her dad with the last of the parcels.

'Just wondering what Brain Damage is up to, that's all.'

Cheryl joined Jamie and her dad in the back room. Kev could hear them going through the list of kids coming for the party.

'Aaron Fowler? Where's his?'

'Over here.'

'Kayleigh Thomas?'

'Hang on, I saw that one a minute ago. Yes, here it is.'

'That's it then,' said Uncle Dave. 'Come on, kids. Home in time for Sunday dinner.'

Kev followed him out into the car park and watched him locking up.

'I just hope nobody knows the burglar alarm's on the blink,' said Uncle Dave. 'The repair man can't come out until Tuesday.'

'Don't go saying that too loud,' said Jamie. 'My nan got broken into last week. Cleared her out they did. A couple of weeks to go before Christmas, and all.'

Kev scanned South Road for any sign of Brain Damage, but the coast was clear. He couldn't help it. Brain Damage's presence had him worried.

'Hello,' came Cheryl's voice. 'Calling Kevin McGovern. Please re-engage on planet Earth.'

'Sorry?'

'You were miles away,' she explained. 'We're ready to go.'

'Oh, right.'

Kev got in the car and slammed the door behind him. As Uncle Dave manoeuvred gingerly on the tightly-packed ice, Kev rubbed at the condensation on the windows.

'It's all right,' said Cheryl. 'He's gone.'

Kev nodded and learnt back against the seat. But just as he was about to relax, he glimpsed a movement by the community centre. It was Brain Damage.

'Hang on, Uncle Dave,' said Kev. 'Brain Damage is still hanging round.'

'That lad? Yes, I saw him earlier.'

Kev was feeling more and more uneasy. One-on-one, he could take Brain Damage any time, but it was what he could get up to behind his back that bothered Kev.

'Why don't you chase him?' he asked.

'I've tried running him off,' said Uncle Dave. 'But he doesn't stay away for long. He'll only come back when we've gone. I'm afraid there isn't much you can do about it. I find the best thing is to avoid antagonising these lads.'

Cheryl laughed out loud. 'Since when?'

'Since I started working here. There are always gangs of lads making a nuisance of themselves. Occupational hazard, I suppose. Forget about him.'

Kev stole a furtive glance at Brain Damage. His arch enemy was looking right at him, a sly grin spreading slowly across his features. Brain Damage was holding something up in his right hand. It was only when they were half-way down South Road that Kev realised what it was.

His watch.

Ten

'That you?'

Kev pulled up short as he closed the front door behind him. It was his mum's voice. She sounded strange. Strange enough to banish his worries about Brain Damage.

'Kev?'

'Yes, I'm coming. Just putting my coat away.'

It was as he reached for the peg that he became aware of somebody standing at the living room door. He didn't need to turn his head to know it wasn't his mum.

'Hello, son.'

'Dad!'

'Bit of a surprise, eh?'

Kev saw Mum hovering in the background. She had a cigarette in her hand. She smoked when she was down. Kev detested the acrid smell in his nostrils. 'I thought you'd given up,' he complained.

She just shook her head and sat down on the couch. Gareth was beside her, looking very small and afraid.

'I should have come earlier,' said Tony McGovern.

Kev had the lines prepared. He'd practised them often enough. *Three years earlier*, he could have said. But he didn't. He stood and stared. There was a thud as his coat hit the floor.

'Aren't you going to pick it up?' his dad asked.

'What?'

'Your coat?'

Kev bent down. His neck was burning. 'Why've you come?' he asked.

Kev watched as his parents exchanged glances.

'It wasn't exactly planned,' his dad began. 'I . . .'

'Me and your dad bumped into each other in the street,' Mum said, interrupting. 'I was clearing the snow, and he was going . . . Hang on a minute, where were you going? Who do you know round here, Tony?'

Kev ran his eyes over the slim, dark-haired man opposite him. He took in the scarred eyebrows and the pinched features.

'I almost fell over her,' Dad went on, dismissing the question. He sounded uncomfortable.

'Why don't we all sit down?' said Kev's mum.

Kev's dad sat, but all the time he was leaning forward on his seat. It was a stranger's way of sitting. 'I bet you're wondering where I've been,' he ventured.

Kev shook his head. His dad was nothing if not a master of understatement. 'You could say that.'

'You're angry.'

Kev stared across the room. He barely understood his own feelings. For so long he had been longing for this moment, but now he felt no warmth towards his dad. Just anger, and a feeling of complete betrayal.

'Noticed, have you?'

'I don't suppose I should have expected anything else.'

'No,' said Kev.

Mum was also sitting forward in her seat, her hand on Gareth's. It was as if Tony McGovern's arrival had made them all strangers to each other.

'Is he really my dad?' asked Gareth from behind Mum's back.

'That's right, son. I'm your dad.'

Gareth shrank even further behind his mum. The last thing he wanted was a direct reply from the unfamiliar figure before him.

'Where *have* you been?' asked Kev.

'Around.'

'That far, huh?' said Kev sarcastically.

'Look,' said Dad, his dark eyes narrowing. 'I know you won't understand how I could clear off like that, but I had no choice.' He glanced across the room. 'I had to go.'

'And I had to stay,' said Kev's mum, meeting his look with cold resentment. 'It's what women do.'

'You didn't write,' said Kev. 'Not even on my birthday.'

'No.'

'Is that all you can say, Tony? No?' Kev watched his mum walk towards her husband. Her body was bent forward and her fists were clenched. 'You'd better go.'

'So what if I don't want to. I'm back now and I want to see my boys.'

'And I want you out of this house!'

Tony McGovern rubbed his chin, then stood up. 'Have it your way, but you won't stop me seeing them, you know. That's if they want to see me.'

With that he walked out. Kev heard the living room door creak, then the sound of footfalls in the hall. His dad's departure seemed to be happening in slow motion, like a dream. Then, as the front door opened Kev darted abruptly to his feet.

'Kev, what are you doing?'

He ran into the street. His dad had almost reached the Ramages' front gate.

'Dad!'

His dad turned.

'Don't go.'

Eleven

'So what's he like?'

Kev gave Jamie a sideways look. He gave the impression of being sore at the whole world.

'Who?'

'What do you mean, who? Your dad.'

'Like my dad.' Only he didn't mean it. His dad was like a stranger.

'Two McGoverns. God help us!'

Normally, that would have set off a bout of play-fighting, but Kev simply trudged on, nursing his suspicions and his worries. He heard a cheery shout.

'Kev, Jamie, heard the news?'

'What's up,' said Jamie. 'Your mum won the lottery or something?'

Ratso shook his head and walked towards them. 'Ronnie's just told us. It's the preliminary round of the Challenge Cup. We've drawn Blessed Hearts.'

'You're joking.'

'Even I wouldn't joke about that.'

Kev watched his mates hurrying towards the community centre car park for a few moments before following. Ronnie was surrounded by the team. They were falling over each other's tongues to quiz the manager.

'Blessed Hearts, you sure?'

'Take a look at the draw sheet if you don't believe me,' said Ronnie.

'It is, and all,' said Ant, staring intently at the piece of paper.

'Grudge match,' said Jimmy.

'Yeah,' said Mattie, 'Showdown time.'

'Demolition job, more like,' said John gloomily. 'And Dave Lafferty will be helping them to take us apart.'

'Lighten up, Johno,' said Ant. 'You don't take a hammering like that every week.'

'No,' said John. 'Just every other week.'

'Give over,' said Ant. 'We don't have to lose. And we've nothing to fear from Dave Lafferty. I talked to him at school. He turned Blessed Hearts down after all.'

'Yes? Why?'

'Loyalty, I suppose. I asked if he wanted to give the Diamonds another go. He's still signed for us.'

'Do you think he will come back?' asked Jamie.

— 118 —

'I'm not sure,' said Ant. 'Do you want me to ask him?'

'What do you think? We need a striker.'

'OK,' said Ant. 'I'll do my best.'

'Anyway,' said Ronnie. 'Are you going to lift this picket line, or what? There'll be no training session without a manager.'

The boys shuffled back to let Ronnie out of his car. Daz was inspecting the draw sheet. 'There's one thing I don't get,' he said. 'How come we have to play a preliminary round?'

'Simple,' said Ronnie, locking the car door. 'We're bottom. There are twelve teams in our division, so the top four teams in the league get a bye.'

'A what?'

'A bye, soft lad,' said Ratso, treating Mattie to a look of contempt. 'They go through without playing.'

'But that's not fair.'

'It's their reward for playing well,' said Ronnie.

'So who goes through?'

Ronnie provided the information. 'Ajax Aintree, Longmoor Celtic, Northend United and St Patrick's Thistle. They're the leading group, so they go straight into the quarter finals.'

'That's right,' said Ratso. 'The other eight teams go into a knock-out round. The four survivors join the top four in the quarter finals of the cup. It's a seeding system.'

Mattie frowned.

'Look at him,' said Ratso. 'I bet he thinks a seeding system's got something to do with keeping budgies.'

'Anyway,' said Ronnie. 'If you want an incentive, take a look at this.' He produced a catalogue. 'I've put an order in for the Brazil strip. This one.'

The team clustered round.

'Imagine wearing that in the final,' said Jamie. 'We'd look brilliant. What do you think, Kev?'

Kev frowned. He'd been brooding about his dad, and what Brain Damage was up to.

'The kit, Kev. Good, isn't it?'

Kev nodded absent-mindedly.

'Can't see us getting far, though,' grumbled John. 'Not with our record.'

Kev at last snapped out of it. 'You're a moaning rat,' he said. 'It's a wonder you expect the sun to rise each day.'

Everybody laughed. Except John.

'He's a right little ray of sunshine,' Kev observed as the boys followed Ronnie on to the mean scrub grass that served as a practice pitch.

'John's all right,' said Jamie. 'He likes a good moan, that's all.'

'So what are we doing, Ron?' asked Ant. 'Not running round the rotten field, I hope.'

Gordon coloured. He didn't like being reminded of his dad's unpopularity.

'A bit of jogging on the spot to warm up,' said Ronnie.

'Aye aye,' said Joey. 'Here's Bash. Late again.'

'It's a wonder,' said John. 'He's going like the clappers.'

'Everything all right, Bash?' asked Kev. 'I called for you, but you were out.'

'Brain Damage has been after me again,' Bashir explained. 'I had to go the long way round to avoid him. He's always hanging round the garages when I go past.'

Kev felt a twinge of anxiety at the mention of Brain

Damage. 'Wait for me and Jamie next time,' he said. 'We *are* mates, remember.'

'OK,' said Bashir. 'I will.'

'Right lads,' said Ronnie. 'In pairs. Trapping, using the underside of the foot.' He walked around, giving advice in a quiet, reassuring voice.

'A bit different to Bobby, isn't he?' said Jamie.

'Not half.'

'That was fine,' said Ronnie. 'Now move a bit further apart. That's it. This time, controlling the ball using the top of the foot. Jamie, knock a hall ball over for Kev. Good take, Kev lad. Now, see if you can all bring it down as well as that.'

Kev and Jamie were shaking their heads at Gordon's attempts to master the skill when they heard a car pulling into the grounds.

'It's your Uncle Dave,' said Jamie.

They gave him a wave then continued with skills practice. Dave Tasker came over and watched them for a while.

'Right lads,' shouted Ronnie. 'Gather round. Let's talk about this Cup game.'

'It's this Sunday, isn't it, Ron?' asked Joey.

'That's right. Our last game before Christmas. It's important for us, boys. We've got our first point under our belt, but it'll do us no good unless we build on it. If we can get our own back on Blessed Hearts, it'll do our confidence a world of good.'

'And take us through to the quarter finals,' said Ratso.

'That's right,' said Ronnie. 'There's not much chance of us winning the league after the start we've had, but we might put together a good Cup run.'

'It's happened before,' said Ratso. 'Like to know when?'

'No,' was the resounding reply.

'So how do we play it?' asked Kev.

'Don't expect any tactical genius off me,' said Ronnie. 'You were starting to create your own system against Fix-It. Tight mid-field. Good breaks from the full-backs and the Daytona demon here . . .' He was pointing at Bashir. 'Bash on the wing.'

'And an attacking goalie,' said Jamie.

'Oh yes,' said Ronnie, giving Daz a playful dig in the ribs. 'A nutter in goal.'

'That it?'

'More or less,' said Ronnie. 'You've got to play your own way. Keep it competitive, run for each other and I think you can turn things round. If we've got one draw-back, it's the lack of a real target-man up front, but goals don't have to come from a striker.'

'Sounds good to me,' said Kev's Uncle Dave. 'Anyway, I've got to open up for the Tenants' Association.'

'See you in a bit,' said Kev.

'Now,' said Ronnie. 'Two groups Relay dribbling.'

Kev was just waiting for Jamie to roll the ball to him when he heard Uncle Dave's voice. It was a cry of dismay.

'Oh no. OH NO.'

'What's up with him?' asked Jamie.

Kev saw the lights go on. A shadow passed over his heart.

'Something wrong?' asked Ronnie, seeing the team staring in the direction of the community centre.

Kev started walking towards the building, then, as he heard another shout from inside, he began to run.

'Uncle Dave, what's wrong?'

He found his uncle in the back room. The *empty* back room. He'd just put the phone down.

'What is it?' asked Ant, catching up with Kev.

'The presents,' Kev replied. 'They've all gone.'

'What sort of people could do this?' groaned Uncle Dave. 'I ask you, a toddlers' Christmas party. It took the Mums and Tots group weeks to raise the money. How am I going to tell them?'

'How did they get in?' asked Ronnie.

'Kicked in a window round the back,' said Uncle Dave.

'Have you phoned the police?' asked Ronnie.

'Yes, just done it. They're on their way.'

The boys had fanned out across the room.

'There's nothing left,' said Bashir. 'Just the wrapping paper.'

'Typical,' said Uncle Dave. 'They can't sell that, can they?'

Kev found himself staring at the wrapping paper they had spent over an hour putting on the presents. He could hear the crunch of car tyres in the car park. Probably the police.

'Do you think it was our friend?' asked Bashir quietly, joining Kev.

'Brain Damage? I wouldn't put it past him.'

'What do you think he's going to do with the presents?' asked Bashir.

'Dunno,' said Kev. 'But I've got a feeling they weren't stolen for money.'

'What then?'

The answer wasn't long coming.

'Hang on,' said Gordon, bending down. 'I think one of the robbers has left something behind.'

'What is it?' asked Jamie.

Kev's heart turned over. It was a watch. His watch.

Gordon turned it over, then stared in disbelief at Kev.

'What is it?' asked Ronnie, taking the watch. 'Good grief!'

Kev felt their eyes on him. He knew exactly what they'd seen. An inscription that read like an accusation.

For you, Kev. You came through.

Twelve

'I don't understand,' said Kev's mum. 'I thought you'd sorted yourself out, now this has to happen.'

Kev was staring fixedly at the tiled floor. 'I haven't done anything wrong.'

'Trouble still seems to follow you though, doesn't it?'

'I told you, didn't I? I never stole anything.'

Mum softened. 'I believe you, son,' she said. 'But will he?'

She nodded towards the policeman who was extending a hand to usher them into the interview room.

'Kevin, Mrs McGovern.'

Kev felt sick. His eyes were red with crying. His mother was in a right state too, just like the time he'd been setting the fires. Crying half the time and chain-smoking the rest. Even while she was telling him she believed him, she still had a look in her eye and a flatness in her voice that cut him to the quick.

Kev listened as the policeman thanked them for coming and explained how the interview would be conducted.

'Now, Kevin,' he began. 'Is this your watch?'

'Yes.'

'Could you explain how it came to be found in South Road community centre?'

Kev shook his head. 'I lost it.'

'When was that?'

Kev muttered that he couldn't remember but his mum gave the information. Kev wondered why she didn't answer all the questions. She'd grilled him often enough over it. It was little wonder that she knew the sequence of events better than he did.

'Did you report it missing?'

Kev lowered his eyes.

'Kevin?'

'No.' He looked at his mum. 'I didn't want my mum to know I'd lost it.'

'And your mum didn't notice it had gone?'

'I got a new one just the same,' said Kev, holding out his wrist. 'I didn't want to let on it had gone. My cousin lent me the money.'

'Your cousin?'

'Cheryl. Cheryl Tasker.'

The policeman wrote down the name. 'And she'll confirm what you've told me?'

'Yes.'

The officer rubbed his chin and glanced over his notes. 'Can you think of any reason the watch might have ended up in the community centre?'

Kev hesitated. He wanted to blurt it out right there and then: *I was set up.*

'I helped my uncle wraps the presents for the kids' party,' he said.

The policeman consulted his notes. 'When was this?'

'Sunday morning.'

'And how long were you there?'

'About an hour. You can ask my Uncle Dave.'

'That'll be Mr Tasker?'

'That's right,' said Kev. 'He's Cheryl's dad.'

'I see. Can you think of anybody who might have broken into the community centre for any reason?'

Kev could feel Brain Damage's name boiling in his throat, but he didn't say it. There was always the same obstacle in the way; the law of the Diamond. You don't grass people up. 'No, nobody.'

'Right,' said the officer, 'That'll be all, Kevin.'

'Is that it?' asked his mum. 'We can go?'

The policeman explained patiently that there was no evidence that Kevin had had anything to do with the break-in.

'So he isn't in trouble?'

'We won't be taking the matter any further, Mrs McGovern,' replied the policeman.

'And that's the end of it?' asked Kev's mum.

'Yes, unless there's anything else you or Kevin would like to tell me.'

The two adults glanced at Kev.

'No,' he said. 'Nothing.'

'Then you can go. Thank you for coming in, Mrs McGovern.'

'Well?'

Uncle Dave was leaning through the open car-window as Kev and his mum emerged from the police station. Aunt Pat was sitting in the passenger seat. Cheryl and Gareth were in the back.

'Nothing,' said Kev's mum. 'They asked Kev a few questions, that's all.'

'So there's nothing to worry about?' asked Aunt Pat.

'It doesn't look like it. I just wish you'd told me about the watch earlier.'

Kev bit his lip. 'Sorry.'

'You didn't help, either,' Aunt Pat told Cheryl. 'Buying him another one. Why didn't the pair of you just tell us it had gone missing? What were you thinking of?'

Kev and Cheryl exchanged glances. 'Sorry.'

'Will you stop saying sorry?' snapped Aunt Pat.

'Oh well,' said Uncle Dave. 'There's no point going on about it. Kev's in the clear. We all know you had nothing to do with it. Squeeze in quick everybody. It's probably illegal to have this many people in the car.'

Kev stood by the car door. Mum pulled Gareth up on to her knee. 'Won't be a sec, love,' she said.

While Kev was waiting to get in, a police car pulled up. He found himself staring as one of the officers got out. His heart leapt.

'Let me in,' he said urgently.

'Don't be so impatient,' Mum scolded.

'Oh, come on,' he pleaded. 'Budge up.'

Kev was trying to keep his face half-turned to avoid the policeman's eyes.

'There. Now you can get in.'

Kev slid gratefully into the back seat next to Cheryl. As the car pulled away he peered out of the window. The policeman was staring back.

'What's up with you?' hissed Cheryl as they reached the first traffic lights.

'Remember when we were looking in Brain Damage's bag?' Kev whispered.

'Yes.'

'Well, that's the copper who chased me.'

Cheryl's eyes widened. Just as Kev was about to say

something else, he noticed his mum frowning at him. 'What's all the whispering about?' she asked.

'Oh nothing,' Kev replied.

It was anything but.

Thirteen

Talk about unwelcome visitors. Fancy you being there when we got back. For a moment I thought Aunt Pat was going to slap your face. I didn't know until today just how much she hated you. How did you hear about the break-in anyway, Dad? Don't tell me. I can guess. I can just hear Brain Damage dropping hints. 'I hear your Kev's been a bit naughty.' Something like that, was it? You might not think being dragged in by the law is such a big deal but Mum does. Telling me not to worry about it, so long as I kept my nerve. Then offering to give me interview tips! You couldn't have upset my mum any more if you'd planned to. It's like you really thought I'd robbed the presents, only you didn't see anything wrong in it. Like you thought I was going to follow in your footsteps.

Then that *copper turned up. Would me and Mum like to attend another interview at South Road police station?*

'You seem to have a funny knack of being in the wrong place, don't you, Kevin?' he said.

I nearly died. My mum's head snapped round like I'd coughed for the whole thing. We had murder after the copper left. Mum went ballistic. She ranted on for hours, grilling me over every little detail until I wanted to scream.

I haven't heard the last of this. Not from Mum for sure. Not from the coppers either.

Fourteen

'What's up?' asked Jamie. 'This isn't our usual training session.'

'You're not here to train,' said Ronnie gravely. 'That's not why I called you over.'

The community centre door creaked. Kev looked up and immediately glanced away again. Gordon had arrived and Bobby was with him. He didn't want to give Bobby the satisfaction of seeing him half-dead with humiliation and worry.

'What then?'

'The break-in.'

Kev's skin began to prickle. He knew some of the boys were staring at him.

'Eh?' said Ant. 'What's that got to do with us?'

'Nothing,' said Ronnie. 'At least, I hope not.'

Kev folded his arms defensively.

'Meaning?' asked Daz.

'Meaning I think we ought to make a little gesture.' Ronnie paused. He was obviously trying to choose his words carefully.

'I don't get it,' said John. 'How do you mean, gesture?'

Ronnie leant forward in his chair. 'I think we ought to let Dave have the money from the sponsored walk. We've had free use of the community centre. It's the least we can do.'

For a moment there was silence. Then Ratso spoke.

'But that means we'll have no kit.'

'That's right,' said Ronnie. 'I want us to put it on

hold. We can't let the kids go without their Christmas party.'

Kev could feel Bobby Jones' presence like an accusation.

'We sweated blood getting that money,' said Ant, aghast.

'That's right,' said Mattie. 'It's not as if any of us nicked those presents.'

Another uncomfortable silence followed, finally broken by Bobby Jones.

'Sure of that, are you?' he asked, turning in Kev's direction.

Kev waited, hoping Ronnie would come to his defence. He didn't. Kev spoke up. 'Ronnie's right. The kids need the money more than we do.'

Jamie shot to his feet. 'You're crazy, Kev. Why should we give up everything?'

'We can make do with the old kit,' said Kev. 'We'll just have to wait a bit longer, that's all. It's different for them. This is their only chance of a party all year.'

'So what's got into you all of a sudden?' demanded John. 'Got something to be guilty about, have you?'

'Come on, boys,' said Ronnie. 'No falling out. It's the right thing to do. Surely we don't need a vote on it.'

Kev could see the look in their eyes. Nobody actually said it, but he knew what they were thinking.

'Oh, give them the rotten money,' said Ant, storming out.

'That's it,' said John. 'This is the last straw. I've had it with this team.'

The exodus into the cold December evening continued until only six of them remained. Bobby and Gordon, Jamie, Bashir and Ronnie. And Kev.

'I could have told you,' Bobby told Ronnie as he

turned to go. 'I knew it would end in tears.' As he closed the door behind him, Kev finally looked up. 'All right, Ron,' he said. 'Let's hear it.'

'I don't know what you mean.'

'Don't come that,' said Kev bitterly. 'You think I did it, don't you?'

'Did I say that?'

'You don't need to.'

'Listen, Kev,' said Ronnie. 'It isn't up to me to judge people. I've trusted you all the way along the line. I still do.'

Words, thought Kev. You're just like all the rest. You think I'm a lost cause. 'It looks like it. So why do we have to hand over the money?'

'For the reasons I gave,' said Ronnie.

'Oh yeah, pull the other one.'

Fifteen

It looks like it's over. The team's dead. John's gone. Maybe Ant as well. Everybody thinks I robbed that stuff, everybody who matters. I'm the licking boy, and that's before I've even had my second interview at the cop shop. Ronnie thinks I did it. He always backed me up, and all. What made me ever think I could keep out of trouble, anyway? What's the point of even trying? There's no way out for the likes of me, is there? Then you turn up. You'll sort it, you say. A new kit will soon have the boys off my back. What makes you so sure?

No, we've had it. I'm a loser, a born loser.

Sixteen

'I thought I might find you here. Your mum said you'd got training in an hour.'

It was Cheryl.

'What do you want?'

'Nothing. I just thought you might need some company.'

'Well, I don't.'

'Nobody thinks you did it, you know.'

Kev gave a humourless chuckle. 'Everybody thinks I did it and I'm up the cop shop tomorrow morning.'

'You've nothing to hide.'

'You're about the only one who thinks so. Jamie and Bashir have given me the benefit of the doubt. That's about it, though.'

'It's Brain Damage,' said Cheryl. 'It's got to be.'

'Tell me something I don't know.'

'So what are you going to do about it?'

Kev shook his head. Cheryl didn't half ask stupid questions! 'There's nothing I can do.'

'You mean you're going to let him get away with it?'

Kev's eyes narrowed. 'I'm not *letting* him do anything.'

'Could've fooled me,' said Cheryl.

'OK, Brain of Britain, tell me what I should do.'

'Well,' said Cheryl, 'If you won't tell the coppers about Brain Damage . . .'

'I can't.'

'Then you've got to find the presents.'

Kev threw his head back. 'Are you for real? I wish it was that easy.'

'I didn't say it was easy,' Cheryl replied. 'But if you won't spill the beans on Brain Damage, it's the only way.'

'You know something,' said Kev, 'you're about as much use as running shoes on a tortoise.'

'I was only trying to help.'

'Suddenly everyone wants to help.'

'What do you mean by that?'

Kev hesitated. 'My dad.'

'Big of him!'

'He thinks he can lay his hands on a kit. Contacts.'

'So how does that help? You can't buy trust.' Cheryl frowned. 'And who are these contacts, anyway? I bet it's Lee Ramage's contacts he means. I wouldn't touch anything he fixed up. Not with a barge pole.'

Kev regretted mentioning his dad's 'job' to her. 'It might get me out of a jam if he could. Everyone's sick about losing the new kit. They think it's my fault.'

'Better no kit, than one paid for by Lee Ramage,' said Cheryl.

'Sometimes,' Kev replied, 'Beggars can't be choosers. It won't come to anything, though. I reckon my dad's all talk . . . Hello, what's this?'

Ronnie had just pulled up in front of the community centre. There was somebody in the passenger seat.

'Bashir!' exclaimed Cheryl. 'I wonder what's going on.'

Bashir was following Ronnie on to the field when he spotted Kev.

'Hang on a minute, Ronnie,' he said.

'What's all this?' asked Kev. 'The training session's not for another half an hour or so.'

'Extra training,' said Bashir. 'Ronnie's been helping me with my crossing.'

'You're kidding. Why didn't you let on?'

'I suppose I was a bit embarrassed really.'

'Are you ready, Bash?' asked Ronnie. Kev had a feeling the manager was avoiding him.

'Yes. I'm coming now.'

'Mind if we hang around for you?' asked Kev.

'Of course not,' Bashir answered. 'We're mates.'

The first of the Diamond players had arrived. They acknowledged Kev with a grudging nod of the head. Kev let it pass without comment.

'He certainly gives up a lot of his time to the team,' said Cheryl, nodding towards Ronnie.

'Yes,' said Kev. 'I wonder why?'

'Dunno,' said Bashir, 'but he's been bringing me up here three days a week.'

'Three!'

'Yes, I was hopeless at first, but I think it's helping.'

Kev nodded. 'You looked pretty good out there.' He suddenly felt hollow inside. He'd been trying to tell himself that Ronnie was just like Bobby Jones, that he wasn't worth a carrot. But Bobby would never have done anything like this. Ronnie really cared about the team. Kev would have given his right arm to have Ronnie's trust. He liked him. He'd thought he could trust him. So why had he given up on the one player who really needed his support? It wasn't Kev's passing that was letting him down, it was his life.

'Anyway, I'm getting off,' said Cheryl. 'I'm going round Helen's.'

'Why don't you watch us train?' asked Kev.

Cheryl wrinkled her nose. 'Not really my scene, Kev. Helen gets my vote. See you.'

If Cheryl had known what was going to happen less than a quarter of an hour later, she mightn't have been so keen to leave. It was a few minutes into the training session that Kev's dad put in his appearance. Kev was glad of the distraction. His team-mates had given him a frosty reception and John hadn't shown. Neither had Dave Lafferty, even though he'd promised Ant and Mattie this would be his comeback night. It all added up to one thing: Kev was about as popular as a Man United fan on the Kop. It wasn't as though anybody actually said anything. That he could have dealt with. It was the way they acted around him, sliding away from him with a sullen glare or pretending not to hear something he'd said.

'Dad, what are you doing here?'

'I told you I'd fix you up with a kit.'

Kev noticed for the first time that his dad was carrying a parcel under his arm.

'Did you say a kit?' asked Jamie. He'd been a bit subdued, but nothing compared to most of the others.

'Yes. Do you want to see?'

'Hey, Ronnie,' shouted Ant. 'Come and take a look at this.'

'What's up?'

'This feller's got us a kit.'

Ronnie clocked Tony McGovern. It was a wary glance. Kev had a feeling Ronnie had been doing his homework on his dad. He clearly didn't like what he'd heard.

'A full kit?' Ronnie asked. 'How much did this set you back?'

Kev tore back the brown packaging and the cellophane wrapper to expose a shirt.

'Nothing,' said Kev's dad.

'Nothing?'

Tony McGovern was enjoying the attention. 'Call it a sponsorship deal,' he said, his reply raising more questions than it answered. As it was obviously meant to.

'But who's sponsoring us?'

Kev's dad tapped his nose with his forefinger. By now Kev was convinced he was doing it on purpose, playing the mystery man. 'You'll see when it's printed on the shirt. Go on, Kev, show the lads.'

Kev held it up. Blue and black stripes.

'Inter Milan,' said Ratso appreciatively. 'Not quite Brazil, but they're good colours. We could wear them with pride. What do you think, Ron?'

'I'm not sure. I'd like to know who's sponsoring us.'

'A local businessman,' said Kev's dad. 'You'll see when we get the name stencilled on the shirts.'

'How long will that take?' asked Jamie eagerly. 'And where's the rest?'

'I've just brought this sample.'

'But will we have them for Sunday?'

'Yeah, it's the Cup game against Blessed Hearts.'

'Now hang on a minute, Jamie,' said Ronnie. 'I haven't agreed to this yet.'

'Come off it, Ron,' said Ratso. 'What's there to agree? We're getting a kit, aren't we? For free, and all.'

'It's not that easy,' said Ronnie.

'It is to me,' said Ant, his hostility to Kev evaporating by the second. 'No kit, no play.'

'Ant's right,' said Joey. 'We've been a joke long enough. This is great. Just what we need.'

'Go on, Uncle Ron,' said Jimmy, applying the emotional thumb-screws. 'Everybody's been really down since we lost the kit money. This is just what we need to lift morale.'

'Yeah, how's about it?'

Ronnie looked around the team. Their tongues were almost hanging out in anticipation of his answer. Ronnie screwed up his eyes, as if concentrating hard on the issue, then nodded. 'OK, we'll take the kit.'

His agreement set off a round of wild cheering.

'Now, back to training. Kit or no kit, we've still got the game to play.'

There was a definite spring in the boys' step as they jogged back on to the pitch. Kev watched them going about their passing with renewed verve. The lay-offs and volleys were crisp and accurate.

'So who *is* sponsoring us?' he asked. He couldn't disguise the uneasiness in his voice.

'You'll see, son. You'll see.'

Kev watched his dad walking back down South Road. He thought about following him. He wanted to discuss the interview with the police. But that's when a familiar sound came to his ears. On the wind he could hear the revving of Lee Ramage's BMW and the *thump, thump, thump* of the car CD player.

PART THREE

The Winner

One

Cheryl was right, after all. I've got to do something. The way that copper looked at me this morning I'm definitely in the frame for the break-in.

You should have heard the questions he was asking me. Don't get me wrong, nothing too heavy. I don't think they're allowed to lean on kids my age too much. He just didn't seem to believe me at all.

Question: Was I there when the bag of stolen goods was found?

Answer: No.

Question: Did I know a policeman had recognised me as one of the group around the bag?

Answer: No (By then I was drowning. What do you say to a question like that?)

Question: Would I like to reconsider my answer?

Answer: OK, so I saw some kids with a bag.

Question: Was it my bag?

Answer: No, I just told you. I saw some kids with the bag.

Question: Did you recognise any of them?

Answer: No.

Question: Did you know what was in the bag?

Answer: No.

And that's the way it carried on, No, No, No. I was scared witless, what with the copper firing his questions and Mum's eyes burning a hole in me. I'd rather have the guy in the black hood and the thumbscrews.

Then just when I thought he was going to keep me all night, the copper told me the interview was over.

Mum wanted to know what was going to happen next, but I don't think she got much joy. It seems to be all statements and stuff like that. I'll tell you what though, the police are not going to let this drop. I know what I'm going to do. Nobody else is going to sort this mess out, so I'm going to do it myself.

Two

There were three of them sitting in a line; Jamie, Bashir and Kev. They had their backs against a half-demolished wall on the corner of Owen Avenue. They seemed oblivious to the biting north-easterly wind that was filling the air with snowflakes.

'What's this?' came a voice. 'The three wise monkeys?'

'Cheryl.'

'Got it in one,' she said. 'Can't pull the wool over your eyes.'

'What are you doing here?' asked Kev.

'Good evening to you, too,' she said sarcastically.

Kev ignored the flip reply and waited patiently for his answer.

'My mum's round yours. Aunt Carol's helping her get her legs waxed.'

'You what?' exclaimed Jamie. 'Like polished, you mean?'

'Don't you know anything?' asked Cheryl. 'It pulls all the little hairs out.'

'You mean she pulls the hairs off her legs?' asked

Jamie, a look of horror creeping over his face. 'Without anaesthetic?'

'Got it in one.'

'Women are weird,' he observed.

'Must be to have anything to do with men,' Cheryl retorted.

'Sharp tonight, aren't you?' asked Kev. 'Been filing your tongue or something?'

Cheryl shrugged her shoulders. 'What happened at the police station?'

Kev glanced at his friends. 'Not much. They just took a statement.'

'That good or bad?'

'How should I know?'

'So what are you doing here?'

'Keeping watch,' said Bashir simply.

'What for?'

'Brain Damage.'

Cheryl looked dismayed. 'Now what are you up to?'

'Nothing.'

'It doesn't sound like it. Look what happened the last time you had a go at Brain Damage.'

Kev picked at his laces. 'So who's having a go at him?'

'Then what *are* you doing?'

'I had an idea,' said Bashir. 'I think I know where he's stashed the presents.' Noticing the accusing glares from his friends, he lapsed into an awkward silence.

'Hang on a minute,' said Cheryl. 'You don't even know for certain it was him.'

'Oh, get real, will you?' said Kev. 'You were saying it was him only last night.'

'Maybe I was,' Cheryl admitted.

'And you said I had to do something.'

—— 143 ——

'Yes, *something*. Like telling the police what you think. But this is stupid. You can't just go steaming in. You'll make things worse and you haven't got many lives left, Kev.'

'I've got to get it sorted,' said Kev dismissively. 'I'm not going to take the flak for something I didn't do. The coppers aren't going to listen. They've got their beady eyes on me. Even some of my mates think I did it.'

'So what are you up to?'

The boys exchanged glances.

'I'm not leaving till I know.'

'There he goes,' said Bashir suddenly.

Cheryl turned. Brain Damage was strolling along the Avenue, swinging that bag in his right hand. Tez Cronin was with him.

'Turn round!' hissed Kev. 'Don't let him know we're taking an interest.'

Cheryl did as she was told. 'What is all this?'

'Promise you'll keep it to yourself,' said Kev.

'Do you even have to ask?'

'Bash worked it out. He always got jumped taking the short-cut home. Always by the garages. It's Brain Damage's stamping ground.'

'So?'

'Well,' said Bashir, 'I got to wondering. What's so interesting about a row of burnt-out garages? Then it came to me. They're not *all* burnt-out.'

Kev was fidgeting nervously. 'Look, do we have to discuss this here? I'm going to follow him.'

'Kev,' said Cheryl. 'Are you sure this is wise?'

'No, but I can't just leave it. He fitted me up. You stay and talk to Bash if you want, but I'm off.'

'Aren't you part of this?' asked Cheryl, as Kev and Jamie moved off in pursuit of Tez and Brain Damage.

'No,' said Bashir. 'I came up with the idea, that's all.'

'What idea? You haven't really told me anything.'

'It's the garages,' Bashir explained. 'Two of them are untouched. Shiny new padlocks and everything. Why?'

Cheryl frowned. She still wasn't sure what he was getting at.

'Don't you see?' said Bashir. Every other garage has been vandalised, but for some reason nobody goes near the two at the end. They daren't.'

'Daren't?'

'Just think about it. If you had to think of somebody whose property would always be safe on this estate, who would it be?'

Bashir paused for Cheryl to reply, but she was clean out of suggestions. 'What about somebody who can park a BMW in Owen Avenue and know it will never even get a scratch?'

'Lee Ramage,' said Cheryl.

'Got it in one,' said Bashir. 'And there's something else. Don't you think it's odd how often he turns up at his mother's house. Maybe it isn't just a family visit.'

'But if Lee Ramage is using the garages surely he wouldn't let Brain Damage near them. He's only a kid.'

'How do you know what Lee lets him do? Maybe Brain Damage doesn't ask. Maybe he sneaks the key or something. All I know is he's always round there, and he's always got that bag with him.'

'So you think it's a lock-up for stolen gear?'

'Don't you?' said Bashir.

Cheryl twisted a lock of hair, turning over the possibility in her mind.

'So, do you think I'm on to something?' asked Bashir.

'Maybe.' Cheryl looked along the road in the direction of the garages. 'I just hope Kev knows what he's doing.'

'Maybe Cheryl's right,' said Jamie.

'What's up?' asked Kev. 'Lost your bottle, like Bash? Got cold feet?'

'No.' Jamie scratched his nose. 'Well, maybe a bit. My mum and dad weren't sure about me knocking round with you in the first place. They'd go hairless if they knew what we were up to.'

'Sh. They're going down to the garages.'

Jamie craned to see over Kev's shoulder. 'What are they doing?'

'I can't see. Hang on, yes I can. Brain Damage is undoing the padlock. Bash was right.'

'What do we do now?'

Kev turned to his friend. 'What do you think? We jump them.'

'You what?'

Kev shook his head. 'What did you think we were going to do? Sing them a flaming lullaby? Are you coming, or what?'

Jamie huddled against the wall. 'I don't like the sound of this,' he said. 'And don't look now, but we're being watched.'

Kev noticed the old lady watching from a window in one of the pensioners' bungalows, then turned on Jamie. 'It's just an old biddy,' he said.

'Old biddies have phones,' Jamies retorted. 'What if she calls the coppers?'

Kev snorted his disgust. He was angry and desperate

at the same time. 'Don't be so spineless. You've got to help me,' he said. 'I thought you were my mate.'

'I *am* your mate,' said Jamie, still casting nervous glances in the direction of the bungalow. 'So's Bash. But I thought we were just going to keep an eye on them and tell somebody about it.'

'Yeah? Well what good do you think watching's going to do us?'

Jamie turned away. 'It's no good, Kev. I'm not going to get into a fight over this.'

Kev was beside himself. 'But they're right there, Jamie. I bet they're looking at the stuff right now.'

Jamie wasn't convinced. He just slumped against the wall, his head bowed.

'All right,' said Kev. 'Have it your own way. I'll sort it myself.'

He started walking towards the open garage door, his steps slowing as he got closer. He could see shadows inside by the dim light of a pencil torch. With a furtive last glance in Jamie's direction, Kev moved in closer. The dull yellow glow of the torch flickered on Brain Damage's face. It's make or break, Kev told himself.

Suddenly, a much stronger beam lanced through the early evening darkness. Kev heard the purr of a powerful car engine behind him. Then the sound of the tyres told him it was swinging on to the tarmac in front of the garages. What's more, Kev recognised it. Not by its sleek lines. He hadn't seen it yet. It was the familiar, pounding beat of the CD system that alerted him.

'Lee Ramage,' he murmured.

The car was close now. He heard the grind of the handbrake. Very slowly, Kev turned. That's when he saw the two occupants.

Sure enough, one *was* Lee Ramage. The other was his dad.

Three

Kev took in the scene at a glance. Tez and Brain Damage emerging from the garage. His dad and Lee Ramage stepping from the BMW. They had left the engine idling and snowflakes were drifting through beam of light.

'Kev?'

His dad was speaking to him, but it was a meaningless noise. Like a loose corrugated sheet scraping against a fence or the ambulance siren whooping in the distance.

'You knew.' Kev was speaking quietly. Little more than a murmur. But the words were barbed.

'You knew,' he repeated.

His father frowned. 'Knew. Knew what?'

Kev felt sick. All along Dad had known about the lock-up. He must have. His own dad and he'd allowed Kev to be dragged in front of the police. For what? A psycho like Lee Ramage. Kev couldn't say another word. He was choking on the truth. He could feel the cold tracks of his own tears on his cheeks. He began to back away. Then the full weight of the betrayal broke on him and he turned and fled.

'Kev,' yelled Dad. 'Kev! What's going on?'

Kev didn't stop. He just ran, his eyes blurring.

'Leave me alone!' he screamed, as he heard his dad's footsteps behind him. 'Just leave me alone.'

Then his father's hands were pinning his arms and turning him round.

'Kev,' he said. 'Stop this.'

'You knew,' sobbed Kev.

His dad looked confused.

'You knew what was in the garages. You knew all the time.'

Kev could see the confusion in his dad's face being replaced by impatience. 'What are you on about?'

'The presents,' yelled Kev.

'Is this some sort of joke:'

'The presents,' Kev repeated. 'The ones Brain Damage nicked from the community centre.'

His dad stared for a moment then turned towards the car. 'I think I'd better have a word with Lee.'

Kev watched from where he was standing as his father walked towards the group by the garages. He saw him talking to Lee Ramage. A noisy exchange with Brain Damage followed, before Lee Ramage finally exploded into a blind rage at his brother.

'You did what, you little blurt? You took my spare key out of the house?'

'I didn't mean anything, Lee. Honest.'

Lee struck the boy a vicious blow across the mouth. A trickle of blood spilled over Brain Damage's jaw and he started sobbing, loud and breathless.

'Maybe that'll teach you to keep your thieving little hands off my things.'

Kev almost laughed out loud. Talk about the pot calling the kettle!

'Here,' said Lee, grabbing Brain Damage by the arm, 'Get this stuff of yours out of my lock-up. Have you got any idea what I've got in here?'

Brain Damage and Tez started carrying the presents out of the garage and into the car boot.

'We'll dump this rubbish later,' said Lee.

'I won't do it again,' Brain Damage snivelled.

'Too right you won't!' snapped Lee. 'Hang on a minute. What's that?'

'Police car!' cried Kev's dad. 'It's the flaming police. Get in the car. I'll have to torch the gear. We can't have this lot traced back to us.'

Kev watched in horror as his dad took a can from the boot and doused the contents of the garage before tossing in a match.

'We're getting out of here,' said Kev's father. 'I think you'd better do the same.' Then he gunned the BMW out on to South Road.

Kev flattened himself against a fence and watched through the slats as it roared away. Seconds later, a police car was racing towards the garages. He was aware of the old lady at the window, craning to follow the car as it sped off. She didn't know he was still there.

'So you phoned the police, did you?' he murmured under his breath.

As the police car screeched to a halt on the approach road to the garages, quickly followed by a fire engine, Kev squeezed through a broken slat in the fence. 'Time to get lost,' he told himself.

At the corner of Owen Avenue he caught sight of Jamie and Bashir waiting for him. He started to run towards them.

Four

They raided the Ramage's house in the early hours of Thursday morning. Drugs and stolen gear they were after, but I reckon that went up in flames in the garages. Half the street were out watching. *Gloating, most of them. You couldn't blame anybody. Talk about the neighbours from Hell!* Tonight's Echo *says they did the same at a house in West Derby. Guess whose? I really put the cat among the pigeons on Wednesday night. I mean, without me starting that row, the old girl would never have called the coppers, would she?*

How do I feel now? How do you think I feel? Just like I always do, ripped in half. I ought to be celebrating, really. I could be the kid who sank the Ramages. Mum says it'll never happen, but you never know. They don't seem too cocky just now. Brain Damage hasn't been in school since it happened. Jamie and Bash keep saying I was dead lucky not to get caught. Maybe I was, but I did something, didn't I?

I actually did something. I don't feel good about it, though. What if my own dad goes down with them? How do I deal with that, sending my dad to jail?

I've been watching every news since Wednesday, my guts churning like I'm going to throw up. I've hardly even thought about tomorrow's Cup game.

Honest to God, I don't know what to think. Somehow, even when I win I'm a loser.

Five

Kev didn't know what to expect. One thing's for certain, he told himself, this game's going to be a bit special. He'd known it the moment he'd walked on to the playing field. For starters, there was actually a bit of a crowd. Not exactly the massed Legions of the Premiership, but not just two dads and a dog either. All the boys' parents seemed to have turned up, and a few other relatives too. Then there was another spicy ingredient – the opposition. Losing again to Blessed Hearts wouldn't be something you could just put down to experience. It would be like chewing on barbed wire. Kev had spotted Luke Costello as he made his way down Jacob's Lane. Old carrot top was arriving in his dad's car. The chance encounter sent the butterflies cascading through his stomach. The slow torture of the earlier nine–nil drubbing scraped agonisingly across his mind's eye. Tension wasn't the word for it. Sometimes Kev wondered why he played football at all. Half the time he didn't even enjoy it. He was angry most of the time. At the opposition, at his team-mates, at himself. He sensed the same charged atmosphere as he walked into the changing rooms. At his entrance the whole place had gone quiet.

'What's up?' he asked.

As if he didn't know. Everybody must have heard about Brain Damage's fall. They would also know he had something to do with it.

'Well?' He said it fiercely, as a challenge. 'Anybody got a problem?'

The watching eyes flicked towards somebody who had just walked in after him. The new arrival was standing somewhere behind his left shoulder.

'That you, Ronnie?' Kev asked, starting to peel off his sweatshirt.

'I think you'd better take a look,' said Bashir quietly.

'Dad! But I thought . . .'

He could feel the other boys' eyes on him.

His father was holding a string-bound parcel in each hand. 'You'll be wanting these,' he said.

Kev stared at the bundles, his brow furrowed.

'Your strip. I told you I'd sort it.'

He opened one bundle and held up the shirt. It was the same Inter Milan kit he'd shown them at the training session. With one change. Across the chest was emblazoned a legend that made Kev's heart turn over. *Ramage*.

'Well, what do you think?'

Kev saw the look on his dad's face. He really fancied himself as the conquering hero.

Ant made a move towards the shirt.

'No,' said Kev, stepping into his path.

'What?'

'Leave them.'

'You're kidding!'

'Come off it, Guv. This is what we've been waiting for.'

'Kev,' his dad said. 'What's got into you?'

Kev pulled his shirt back on. 'Let's talk outside.' Then, as he reached the door. 'And nobody touches that kit. Got it?'

Kev faced his father in a lonely corner of the car park. 'You don't think we're going to wear that, do you? After what's happened?'

'Don't believe everything you read in the papers,' said Kev's dad. 'Lee's in the clear. The police have got nothing on him. Released after questioning. He's a legitimate businessman.'

'Oh yeah, and I'm Alan Shearer,' Kev scoffed. 'What you mean is, the evidence has gone up in flames. So what sort of business is he supposed to have?'

'Motors,' said his father. 'He owns a garage on Breck Road.'

'You must think I'm stupid,' said Kev. 'You forget. I

know all about his garages. Anyway I'm not wearing that low-life's colours. I'd have sold myself to him.'

His dad's face blazed with anger. 'Is that what you think of me?'

Kev looked away, his gaze fastening on the wind-blown litter that was heaped against the perimeter fence. 'You said it.'

'Well,' his dad sighed. 'Have it your own way.'

Kev hated his own hardness, but he knew it was the only way. It was just about the most difficult thing he'd ever had to say, but he said it. 'Take them with you, Dad.'

'You sure?'

'I'm sure.'

Tony McGovern started to walk towards the changing rooms. He stopped after a few steps.

'You must really hate me, Kev.'

'No,' Kev answered. 'That's the trouble.'

His dad gave a half-smile.

'Dad,' Kev ventured. 'You don't need Lee Ramage. Why don't you stay and watch me play?'

'Better not, eh?' said his dad. 'I've got my way to survive and you've got yours. See you around, son.'

Looking at the hard, wasted man in front of him, Kev wanted to shake him. To somehow make him see he was throwing his life away. But he knew he would be wasting his breath.

'Yes, see you, Dad.'

Kev waited for a couple of minutes to give him a chance to leave. Or maybe it was to hide how he felt. Then he walked inside.

'You barmy, or what?' John O'Hara started in on him.

'Meaning?'

'You gave it back. That's the second strip we've lost. What's your game, McGovern? Do you have to screw up everything you touch?'

There was a time that kind of language would have lit the blue touch-paper, but Kev was determined to handle it. He'd had a let-off with the police and he wasn't about to blow it again. To everybody's surprise he took the tongue-lashing coolly. 'Some things are more important than what you wear on your back,' he said. 'If we took Ramage's colours, it wouldn't matter what the score was. We'd still be losers. Right now, I don't care if we wear pink and purple with yellow spots. We can still beat Blessed Hearts.'

'Oh yeah!'

'The boy's right,' said a familiar voice. Ronnie had arrived.

'Cutting it fine, aren't you, Ron?' observed Jamie.

'I had to pick something up on the way.'

'Come again?'

'These.'

Ronnie was holding up a pair of string-bound bundles.

Kev's face drained of blood. He couldn't believe his dad had stooped so low. Asking Ronnie to try again. 'They go back!' he cried.

'I beg your pardon?'

'I've told my dad already. And it's no use him trying to use you to sell the kit to us. We don't want it. We don't want anything from Lee stinking Ramage.'

'Who said anything about Lee Ramage?' asked Ronnie, defending his parcels from Kev's flailing arms. 'This is the kit I had on order. The one you all chose together.'

'What?'

'You lot gone deaf or daft? This is your Brazil strip.'

'But . . .'

'Do I have to spell it out for you? The police have recovered the presents for the kids' party. They found them strewn across waste-ground at the back of South Parade. It can go ahead as planned, so Dave didn't need the cash we offered him. Simple.'

'I don't get it,' said John.

'No,' said Ratso. 'You wouldn't.'

Kev watched as Ronnie tore open the wrapping paper and produced the stunning Brazil shirt.

'What's up?' asked Ronnie, still unaware of Tony McGovern's visit. 'Have you gone off it?'

The remark was met with laughter. Then just as it was subsiding, somebody else made their entrance.

'Well, well,' said Ronnie. 'Dave Lafferty as I live and breathe. And just when we all thought you'd given up on us.'

'Do I get a game, or what?' asked Dave.

'Yes, you're in. We need a goal poacher.'

'Hey,' said Dave pouncing on one of the shirts. 'Nice kit. How did you get your hands on this?'

At that the laughter resumed, only twice as loud.

'Did I say something funny?' asked Dave.

'Yes,' said Kev. 'Dead funny.'

'Ready for another hammering?' asked Jelly Wobble. 'It could go into double figures this time.'

'Give it your best shot,' said Kev. 'We're ready for you.'

'You sure about that?' asked Jamie, as Jelly Wobble stalked away.

'Ready as we'll ever be,' said Kev. 'We've got the name, we've got the colours.' He inspected the crisp, golden shirt on his chest. 'And we've got the music.' He paused. 'At least I thought we had. Where's Ratso?'

He scanned the crowd that had spread along the touch-line. Uncle Dave was there.

'Hi, Dave,' Kev said cheerily. 'Why didn't you tell us you were giving back the kit money?'

'I thought you'd have figured that out for yourself,' said Dave. 'A bright lad like you.' What is this, thought Kev, good news *and* compliments!

'Cheryl with you?'

'Yes, she's just coming. We've another couple of your fans in tow, as well.'

That's when Kev saw them. His mum and Gareth squeezed past John O'Hara's mum and dad and took their places beside Dave.

'I thought you didn't like football,' said Kev.

'I don't,' his mother said. 'But that's not why I'm here, is it?'

Kev smiled self-consciously. 'Seen anything of Ratso, anyone?'

His question was interrupted by a deafening blast of *Gangsta's Paradise*.

'It's all right,' said Kev. 'I think we've found him.'

'Good choice, Rats,' said Jamie, doing his rapper impression.

'I was going to pick *Saturday Night's all right for fighting*,' Ratso told him. 'What with it being a bit of a needle match, and all.'

'So why didn't you?' asked Ant. 'Too provocative?'

'No,' said Ratso. 'I dropped it because it's Sunday, divvy. It would have sounded stupid.'

The ref blew his whistle for the match to start.

'Hey, Bash,' said Kev. 'Ready to show off your new skills?'

Bashir gave a shrug of the shoulders.

'What's up?'

'Leave him,' said Jamie. 'He's nervous.'

He had reason to be. Blessed Hearts pressed right from the kick-off. They were determined to bury the Diamonds. Their tackling was hard bordering on the dirty, and when it came to Dave Lafferty it crossed the boundary. Every time he got the ball he was treated to a crunching tackle.

'You all right, Dave?' asked Kev.

'Yes, fine,' said Dave hobbling away. 'I should have expected it, I suppose. They think I'm some sort of traitor because I didn't play for them. Still, at least it might take a bit of the heat off you, Guv.'

It was a vain hope. Ten minutes into the game, Kev had started to work the first promising opportunity when Luke Costello came in with a two-footed tackle. Kev crumpled, holding his ankle.

'Come on, ref,' howled Ant. 'Give us some protection, will you?'

The protest earned Ant a steely glare from the official.

'Flaming typical!' he grumbled, offering Kev a helping hand. 'They crunch us and we get told off for complaining. What gives?'

'Didn't you hear what happened before the kick-off?' asked Joey Bannen.

'No, I was talking to the family.'

'It seems the proper ref's ill. There was a toss-up between Ronnie and the Blessed Hearts' manager for who should referee the game.'

'So you mean that's their manager?' asked Kev, appalled.

'Got it in one.'

'Oh, wonderful!'

Worse was to come. Jelly Wobble had the ball on the edge of the Diamonds' box. He worked a one-two and shoved the return ball past Jimmy Mintoe. Jimmy recovered well and slid the ball clear. That's when it happened. Stumbling over Jimmy's outstretched leg, Jelly Wobble crashed theatrically to the ground.

'Seen the kip of him?' chuckled Mattie Hughes. 'Dying swan act, or what?'

The referee soon wiped the smile off his face. Without a moment's hesitation, he pointed to the spot.

'Aw, ref,' Ant complained bitterly. 'You've got to be joking.'

'I've already spoken to you, haven't I?' asked the ref. 'Consider yourself booked.'

Kev saw the warning signs. If Ant kept it up the Diamonds would be down to ten men by half-time.

'Come away,' he ordered, tugging at Ant's shirt.

'Why?' Ant demanded. 'That was no penalty. The ref's blind.'

'OK,' said Kev. 'So I'll buy him a white stick for Christmas. Now just drop it, will you?'

Ant grudgingly accepted the guiding hand and trailed to the edge of the box. Jelly Wobble placed the ball on the spot, took a three step run-up and hit it to Daz's left. Daz dived well and pushed the ball on to the post, only to see it cannon back into the net. One–nil.

'Hard luck, Daz,' said Kev. 'You nearly had that.'

Daz just glared at him. As far as he was concerned, conceding a goal was a personal insult. Sympathetic words just made it worse.

'Come on, Diamonds,' shouted Kev. 'Shake your-selves. We haven't got into gear yet.' He saw Bash lonely out on the left wing. He'd hardly had a touch of the ball.

'Dave,' he called. 'To me.'

Kev took the ball forward. He kept his eye on the opposition defence, expecting more rough handling. This time the tackle was telegraphed. Kev hurdled the sliding tackle, skipped past a second player and laid it off to Bashir. A third tackle felled him after the ball was gone, but he wasn't complaining. It had done the trick. Bashir was free. He had no trouble losing his marker, but the real challenge was still to come. Luke Costello was pounding in. He didn't look in the mood for taking prisoners.

'Bash,' yelled Kev. 'Get rid of it.'

He didn't care where. He just wanted to protect his friend. He needn't have worried. Bash checked, pulled the ball back on his instep and left Costello for dead. Appreciative laughter ran through the spectators.

Kev was on his feet by then, racing towards the box to get involved in a promising move.

'Bash,' screamed Ant. 'My ball.'

He was close to Bashir, offering to cross it for him. Bashir just shook his head and took it to the line.

'Bash,' yelled Ant. 'You'll never get it over from there.'

But he'd reckoned without Ronnie's nights of coaching at South Road. Bash sent over a looping cross that dropped threateningly towards Hearts' far post.

The keeper gave a despairing dive and scooped it off the line, only to see it drop invitingly in Dave Lafferty's path. Dave struck a stunning volley right across goal and into the far corner.

One–all.

'Bash,' Ant said to the astonished winger. 'That was brilliant. I didn't know you had it in you.'

'No,' said Bashir humbly. 'Neither did I!'

The Diamonds' goal seemed to set a fire under both teams. For ten minutes all the action was in mid-field as both sides crashed in with ferocious tackles.

'It can't go on like this,' said Jimmy. 'Somebody's going to get their leg broken.'

'So long as it's one of them,' said Kev grittily. He'd definitely had it with losing.

It was Dave Lafferty who finally conjured something out of the confusion. Chipping the ball cleverly over his marker, he moved out on to the right, spreading the Hearts' defence. Kev immediately made a run, taking two Hearts' defenders with him. That's when Dave released the ball.

'Where the hell's he putting that?' groaned John, positive as usual.

'There,' said Kev.

The long cross-field pass had found Bashir.

'Get on him!' shrieked Luke Costello, seeing the danger.

Bashir rolled the ball forward as he sized up the state of play. Then, with barely a hint of back-lift, he swung a cross into the area. Sensing another chance, Kev started to jog into the area where Dave was rising to meet the in-swinging ball. It was the coolest of headers, taking the pace off it and dropping it neatly into the danger area. Suddenly Kev knew it was his. He pounded in, holding off the nearest defender and stuck out a leg.

'Goal!' came the united cry.

Except for Ratso, who peeled away on an aeroplane run. 'Goooooaaaalll!'

As for Kev, he was sprinting towards the touch-line, fists raised, snarling his joy. He found himself facing Bobby Jones, who'd just arrived. 'Does the face fit yet?' he demanded. 'Does it, Bobby?'

It certainly fitted with Ronnie. He met them beaming as they came off at half-time. 'Brilliant, lads. Two–one up and you deserve it. More of the same in the second half.'

'Is that it?' asked Jamie. 'That the team-talk?'

'That's about it,' Ronnie answered. 'There's only one thing that worries me.'

'So what's that?' asked Kev.

'Don't get me wrong,' said Ronnie. 'The mid-field work is great, the attacking breaks have been lethal.'

'But?'

'But we look slow at the heart of our defence. They haven't exploited it yet, but they could. The Costello boy's got pace. Anybody got anything to say?'

Ronnie seemed to have picked out Mattie Hughes. Mattie shook his head.

'OK, like I said, same again.' The boys were about to go when Ronnie spoke again. 'Kev,' he said. 'Hang on a second.'

'What's the matter?'

Ronnie made sure nobody was listening. 'I think I owe you a bit of an apology, lad.'

Kev shook his head.

'No,' said Ronnie. 'Don't argue. I was half-starting to believe what Bobby said about you. I was wrong.'

'Forget it.'

'I can't,' said Ronnie. 'I ought to have backed you all the way. I should have known better.'

'Meaning?'

'I've been through this before. You know, seeing a

good lad getting drawn into trouble. My own boy Michael got a bit wild in his teens. I suppose I stood aside and watched. I was hoping he'd grow out of it. He didn't. One night he and his mates were messing on a warehouse roof. Mike slipped and fell through a skylight. He's in a wheelchair now. I suppose that's why I spend so much time with Jimmy and the rest of you lads. I want to make sure you boys don't make the same mistakes as our Mike.'

Kev didn't know what to say.

'You're all right, Kev,' said Ronnie. 'Follow your conscience, lad, and you'll do just fine. Go on, win us the match.'

But after the break the play didn't go according to plan at all. Blessed Hearts had reorganised, with Luke Costello playing deeper and challenging for the ball.

'What's going wrong?' asked Jamie as Daz saved the Diamonds from an early equaliser.

'It's Costello,' said Kev. 'Since he came into midfield they've got a man over.'

'So what do we do?'

'Good question,' said Kev. 'We pulled out all the stops in the first half.'

Costello was the playmaker again in the next Blessed Hearts attack, stroking the ball into Jelly Wobble's path. It was one on one with Mattie Hughes.

'Close him down, Matt,' cried Kev.

It was no use. Jelly Wobble left Mattie for Dead. Daz came out, spreading himself, but Jelly Wobble was no mug. He just stabbed it along the ground, the worst place for a tall lad like Daz. Two–all.

It was the same story from the re-start as Luke Costello dispossessed Bashir on the left. Mattie's tackle was utterly lacking in conviction and Costello struck the ball across the face of the goal.

In the scramble that followed, the ball hit Joey Bannen on the shin. Two–three. Suddenly the whole shape of the Diamonds team seemed to be falling apart.

Kev found himself looking across at Ronnie.

'What's the matter, Kev?'

'You were right, Ron. Central defence is the problem. I think Mattie's carrying an injury.'

'I thought as much. He's off. Gordon, get your trackie off.'

Kev stared in disbelief. 'Gord? Why not Carl?'

Ronnie greeted the question with a stern frown. 'Gord I said and Gord I mean. Any disagreements?'

Kev shook his head, but for the first time, he was having doubts about the manager's sanity.

'What's Ronnie playing at?' groaned John.

'I don't know,' said Kev. 'But it isn't football.'

Ronnie raised the fingers of two hands to signal the time remaining.

'Ten minutes, lads,' shouted Kev, collecting the ball from Daz's long throw.

He was looking for options when he was clattered from behind. Costello. Ant was immediately on the scene.

'You're an animal, Costello. You belong in a zoo.'

'So where does *he* belong?' demanded Costello, glaring at Kev. 'Tell me that. At least I never burned anyone.'

'Leave it,' Kev told Ant. 'Just forget it. He isn't worth the trouble.'

Jamie was standing over the ball, waiting to take the

free-kick. 'I don't believe it,' he said. 'Is this really the Guv'nor speaking?'

'It's me, all right. Now listen, Jamie. They've got the beating of us in mid-field and now we're carrying Gordon, so just get it up front. Long balls, anything.'

Jamie nodded and knocked it out to Jimmy who was making a break on the right. Unfortunately, it was over-hit and ran out of play. From the throw-in Costello made a strong run through the middle. Until he came up against Gordon.

'Gord Almighty!' breathed Kev. 'Did you see that, Jamie?'

Jamie had and so had the rest of the team. Gordon had robbed Costello with a beautifully-timed sliding tackle.

Kev turned towards Ronnie for an explanation.

'Bashir's not the only one I've been giving extra training,' he said with a broad smile.

Gordon checked and laid the ball off to Ant. Ant found Jimmy and he, in turn, found Bashir.

The Diamonds were putting their passing game together. Bashir set off on another run, but this time Hearts were ready. Two of their biggest boys sand-wiched him.

'Aw, ref!'

Even this ref couldn't overlook such a blatant foul. It was a free kick on the edge of the box.

'My ball,' said Dave.

'Says who?' Jamie retorted. 'Guv takes the best free kicks.'

Kev gave Dave a querying look.

'I want it,' Dave told him simply. 'I think I owe them one.'

Kev understood. He could feel Dave's anger and determination. 'Dave's ball,' he said.

He watched Dave pace out his run up, then hit it with his instep. It was a terrific strike but fortune took a turn. The ball glanced off Costello's shoulder as he tried to charge down the shot. The Hearts' keeper had no chance. The change of direction left him floundering and the shot cracked against the underside of the cross-bar before bouncing over the line. Three–all. 'Hey, nice assist, Costello,' Kev taunted.

But the red-haired Hearts' captain wasn't finished yet. From the kick-off he sent the right winger away with a long pass and ran on to take the return pass. Seeing the danger, Daz came off his line, only for Costello to take it round him. With the goal at his mercy, Costello side-footed it and peeled away to celebrate. But there was no goal.

'Gord Almighty!' was the roar from the Diamonds. Gordon's long leg had slid it just the wrong side of the post for a corner.

'Where did he come from?' demanded Costello bitterly.

'Heaven,' said Ratso blissfully.

'Two minutes, lads,' said Kev, taking the near post. 'Ronnie's given me the signal.'

'Two minutes?' said Daz. 'Time for my party piece.'

'We've got to keep this corner kick out first,' said Kev.

Daz was off his line the moment the outswinger came over. To everybody's amazement he didn't catch it. Instead he chested it down and followed the bounce of the ball out of his area.

'He's cracked,' said Ant. 'He's rotten well cracked!'

'Who cares?' said Kev. 'He's split their defence wide open. Get after him.'

By now Daz had powered into the Hearts half of the field. Even Ronnie was screaming for him to get back in goal.

'Daz,' yelled Kev. 'Pick out Bashir.'

Daz didn't need telling twice. Releasing the ball to his left, he bent double.

'And you wonder why I like it in goal,' he panted. 'I've got a stitch.'

Out on the left, Bashir was facing two defenders. Kev and Dave both made runs for him. Bashir chose Dave.

'Dave,' yelled Kev, only to hear a much louder shout behind him.

'Dave!'

Daz's adventure up-field wasn't over. He met Dave's cross perfectly and headed it past the keeper's flailing arms . . . only to hit the post.

'I don't believe it!' said Kev, racing after the ball. He glimpsed a red blur to his left. Costello. It was between the two of them. For a moment Kev thought he was going to lose out, then he saw his dad behind the goal. So he hadn't gone. With a desperate lunge, Kev pulled back the ball and turned. The move beat Costello whose movement carried him over the line.

'Guv,' shouted Dave.

'Guv,' cried Daz.

But Kev had spotted the Hearts' keeper off his line. If he got it right, he could hit the ball inside him at the near post. Without a moment's hesitation Kev struck it. It was the sweetest moment he'd ever tasted in football. The ball rose like a rocket and hit the roof of the net. Kev punched his fist into the air. Goal! Suddenly there was only one thing to do. The shirt had to come off. It was celebration time. Kev dodged his team-mates and peeled away, swinging his shirt in his right hand.

'Get that shirt back on, lad,' shouted the ref.

But Kev wasn't listening. He ran the length of the touch-line, waving his colours.

Within a minute the match was all over. The Diamonds were through to the quarter-finals. Four–three.

'Hey Costello, Jelly Wobble,' Kev taunted as they trailed away. 'So what's the score now?'

But they didn't answer.

'What's up? Cat got your tongue?'

Still no answer. They were choked.

'That was brilliant,' said his mum.

'Yeah,' Cheryl added, 'You came through after all.'

'I did, didn't I?' said Kev. 'Has anybody seen my dad?'

'Don't get your hopes up,' said his mum. 'He's never going to change.'

'What do you mean? Have you seen him?'

She hesitated, then turned slowly. 'Over there.'

Kev saw his dad standing at the entrance to the sports ground. For a moment he looked down the road then crossed towards a waiting car. Kev watched in disbelief. It was Lee Ramage's BMW.

'What's he doing?' cried Kev.

He felt his mother's hand on his arm. He looked away from her. His eyes were stinging.

'I don't know,' she said. 'Looks like he'll never learn. You did though, didn't you, Kev?'

Kev nodded sadly. He was a winner all right, and he was going to stay that way. But it didn't stop him hurting inside. There was a question nagging in his brain, the sort of question you spend a lifetime trying to answer. How come even when you win, part of you still has to lose?

Rough Diamonds

THE SQUAD

Darren 'Daz' Kemble (goalkeeper)
Joey Bannen (defence and substitute goalkeeper)
Mattie Hughes (defence)
Anthony 'Ant' Glover (defence)
Jimmy Mintoe (defence)
Carl Bain (defence)
John O'Hara (mid-field)
Jamie Moore (mid-field)
Kevin 'Guv' McGovern (mid-field)
Bashir Gulaid (mid-field)
Pete 'Ratso' Ratcliffe (mid-field)
Dave Lafferty (striker)
Gordon Jones (striker and captain)

Manager: Bobby Jones